Mr. Darcy

broke

my heart

BETH PATTILLO

Guideposts
New York, New York

Mr. Darcy Broke My Heart

ISBN-13: 978-0-8249-4793-4

Published by Guideposts
16 East 34th Street
New York, New York 10016
www.guideposts.com

Distributed by Ideals Publications, a division of Guideposts
2636 Elm Hill Pike, Suite 120
Nashville, Tennessee 37214

Guideposts and *Ideals* are registered trademarks of Guideposts.

The characters and events in this book are fictional, and any resemblance to actual persons or events is coincidental.

Library of Congress Cataloging-in-Publication Data

Pattillo, Beth.
  Mr. Darcy broke my heart / Beth Pattillo.
    p. cm.
  ISBN 978-0-8249-4793-4
  1. Americans—England—Fiction. 2. Austen, Jane, 1775–1817. Pride and prejudice—Fiction. 3. England—Fiction. I. Title.
  PS3616.A925M7 2010
  813'.6—dc22

                        2009039525

Cover design by the DesignWorks Group and Georgia Morrissey
Cover art by Trevillion Images
Interior design by Lorie Pagnozzi
Typeset by Nancy Tardi

Printed and bound in the United States of America

10 9 8 7 6 5 4 3 2 1

FOR MY EDITOR,

BETH ADAMS,

FOR HER PATIENCE, SUPPORT, AND WISDOM.

"Seldom, very seldom, does complete truth belong to any human disclosure; seldom can it happen that something is not a little disguised, or a little mistaken."

—Jane Austen

he taxi pulled up outside Christ Church and I climbed out of the backseat, but the scorching July heat stole my breath and threatened to press me back inside the cab. I swiped at the sweat dripping down my forehead and righted myself on the pavement. When my sister talked me into taking her spot in a summer seminar on *Pride and Prejudice*, I'd expected the dreaming spires of Oxford, intellectual conversation, and long walks along the tranquil river. I hadn't expected to arrive soaked with perspiration and deeply in need of a shower, all because of my sister's obsession with one Fitzwilliam Darcy.

The gateway beneath Tom Tower, Christ Church's main entrance and one of its most distinctive features, would have looked at home with a drawbridge and a moat. A portcullis at a minimum. But the modern inhabitants of the college had made do with some wrought iron as their lone defense against the real world. I paid the driver and wrestled my suitcase from the taxi. It landed on the ground next to me with an ominous thud. I squared my shoulders, took a very deep breath, and moved forward, sweat trickling down my spine.

"Good morning." A spry middle-aged man in some sort of uniform stepped forward. "Welcome to Christ Church."

He motioned me through the gate, which led to a passage cut through the building itself. It was a good fifteen feet across and paved in cobblestones. To the left was some kind of office. A sign identified it as the Porters' Lodge.

"Thank you." I paused, unsure where to go.

"Straight through and to the left. You'll see the registration table." His face was weathered, but his chipper tone and bright blue eyes spoke of abundant energy. He winked. "Just leave your case here, and someone will take it to your room. Enjoy your stay."

Enjoy my stay? I swallowed the bark of laughter in my throat. I was here under duress, against my better judgment, and out of desperation. Enjoyment might be too lofty a goal.

I followed the porter's instructions and stepped out of the cool shadow of the gateway into Tom Quad, the heart of the college itself. The walls of the buildings formed a large, open square in front of me, an arena of golden stone punctuated by elegant arches, wooden doors, and mullioned windows. On the opposite side I could see the entrance to the cathedral that gave the college its name, and a raised, paved walkway that formed a square of its own just inside the walls. In the center of the quad, gravel walks crisscrossed, with an elegant fountain, complete with a statue of Mercury, at their meeting point.

Christ Church. The holy of holies within Oxford University. And the last place on earth I'd ever have thought to find myself.

That thought renewed the panic that had been lodged in my stomach since I boarded the plane for Heathrow. I turned to my left as the porter had directed and mounted the few steps onto the walkway. My sandals tapped against the pavement, made of the same weathered stone that formed the walls, and the sun beat down on my head.

I had read that the other colleges within Oxford had cloisters or covered walkways, but Christ Church had run short of funds during construction, and the cloisters had never been completed. Now I felt as exposed as those walkways. No shade, no shelter, no covering. Just me. An unemployed former office manager with a GED, a sports-obsessed boyfriend who might not have noticed that I'd left the country, and a perilously empty bank account.

No point in panicking right now, I lectured myself as I approached the registration table, a smile pasted on my face. *You have at least a week until you have to figure out what to do with the rest of your life.*

The thought was not particularly comforting.

❦❦❦❦❦

A steaming cup of tea hardly seemed the best choice for a torrid July morning, but that was all that was on offer in the Junior Common Room. I'd picked up my participants' folder from an eager, rather pierced student at the registration table and followed her instructions to walk farther along the quad to the student lounge.

I took the cup of tea from the smiling woman behind the pass-through and looked down the length of the room at the assortment of unoccupied chairs and tables. In my eagerness to arrive, I'd made the mistake of showing up too early. The last thing I wanted was to look like a desperate wannabe.

I settled at a table next to the windows that overlooked St. Aldate's Street and tried to look as if I belonged there. My sister Missy had received a grant to attend this weeklong seminar in Oxford as part of her continuing education for her teacher certification, but pregnancy complications had kept her from traveling, and here I was instead.

Missy had assured me I'd love it. A lot of people came to Oxford and took these courses just for fun, she said. All I had to do was take notes and present her paper, and Mr. Harding would count it toward her in-service hours. The principal of Missy's school had been extremely accommodating. So had I, because here I was, a fish out of water on the other side of a really big pond.

The folder the young woman handed me was thicker than I'd expected. *Joining Notes.* I leafed through its contents as I waited for my tea to cool to the point where it wouldn't burn my tongue. Pages and pages of instruction on how and where to conduct myself while at Christ Church. Be on time for classes and meals. Jackets and ties for gentlemen invited to dine at the head table. Use of the Master's Garden, normally reserved for faculty, was included as part of our program, as was access to the famous Bodleian Library.

Then there was information about Oxford. A map of the college and its environs. And, finally, a list of attendees.

I scanned the page, which listed all the participants in the different seminars being held that week. As I read, my stomach tightened into a series of knots that rivaled my late mother's attempts at macramé. Next to each name was listed "Occupation." I'd known I was going to be out of my league, but I'd had no clue just how far. Several doctors, even more lawyers. Stockbrokers. Professors. A couple of business owners. A judge. Participants who viewed the combination of education and travel as a recreational activity. By the time I made it to the bottom of the list, I was thoroughly intimidated. There, at the bottom, was my sister's name. Missy Zimmerman. Teacher.

I swallowed the sigh of relief that rose in my chest. As a last-minute substitute, I wasn't listed. Nowhere on the paper did it say Claire Prescott, Unemployed Pediatrics Office Manager with No College Degree.

And then the realization hit. No one here knew anything about me. For the next week, I could be anyone or anything I wanted to be.

I blew on my tea to cool it as the idea took root in my mind. The temptation was overwhelming. For more than thirty years, I'd always been exactly who people needed me to be. A dutiful daughter. An even more dutiful big sister. A hard worker, so I could provide for Missy after our parents died, put her through college, and pay for her wedding. A devoted aunt to my twin nieces. I had never objected to being any of those things or playing any of those roles. But I had never chosen them either.

A sudden movement to my right pulled my attention from the list in front of me. I looked up and saw a tall, dark-haired man framed in the doorway of the Junior Commons.

Thank goodness I didn't have the cup of tea in my hand at that moment. I jerked as if I'd just touched a hot stove. Every bit of oxygen in my lungs disappeared. It was only by some stroke of luck that I didn't slide to the floor beneath the table in a faint. More sweat beaded on my forehead, but this time it had nothing to do with the heat.

Whoever he was, he was the handsomest man I'd ever seen in my life. He took two steps into the room and surveyed the paltry occupants. An older gentleman, probably retired, sat by the door. A young man with floppy blond hair and white earbuds lounged in the corner. And then there was me.

To my surprise, he crossed the room until he was standing next to my table. Clearly I was the least of the three evils in the room.

"Do you mind if I join you?" he asked.

I slid my cup and saucer over. "Sure. I mean, no. I mean…" I stopped before I could embarrass myself further.

"I'll take that for a yes." At first I thought he was teasing me, but he didn't smile. He lowered himself from his considerable height into the chair next to me, and my heartbeat accelerated even more. "James Beaufort," he said with a nod.

"I'm Claire Prescott." I didn't know whether to extend my hand, but since he didn't offer me his, I gripped the handle of my cup instead.

He glanced around the room. "Not much of a crowd so far."

"No." Now my tongue had as many knots in it as my stomach did. Why in the world had he chosen to sit by me? I tried to think of some brilliant conversation starter. "The tea's very good, though." Okay, not exactly brilliant.

He glanced down at his cup. "Too strong." He dismissed my opinion, and I cringed. He wasn't the most pleasant man I'd ever met. A shame, given that he had the face of an angel beneath that dark, wavy hair.

"Have you been to Oxford before?" I asked. The question was the one surefire opening gambit I'd thought up on the plane.

"No, I haven't."

A dead end. "Me either."

After that fruitless exchange, silence descended, snuffing out any hope of a conversational flame. I sipped my tea, even though it burned my tongue, and wondered why in the world he didn't get up and go find more interesting company. In desperation, I turned back to the *Joining Notes* and started to reread them.

"Where are you from?"

His voice startled me. Fortunately my cup wasn't quite so full anymore.

"Kansas City." Even as I answered, I knew how boring it sounded. Most people thought of my hometown as a stockyard that happened to have some houses in the vicinity, when in reality it was a lovely place, with wide, curving boulevards and elegant fountains. "What about you?"

"Manhattan." Not New York City. Much more specific. And much more expensive.

"What do you do there?" If I glanced at the sheet on the table in front of me, I could find out for myself, but at least it gave us something to talk about.

"I'm in publishing. Family business."

"Oh." Ivy League, no doubt. Probably only read Nobel Prize-winning literature and biographies that could double as doorstops.

I lowered my gaze again. Just looking at him made my teeth hurt, he was so yummy. How unfair that such a beautiful man couldn't be more pleasant.

"Which seminar are you attending?" I asked. There were six or seven occurring simultaneously during the week. I pegged him for continental philosophy. Or the ruins of Roman Britain.

"*Pride and Prejudice.*" He didn't look too happy about it.

My eyebrows shot up. "Me too."

He scanned the list of participants. "I don't see your name here."

"It's not, actually. I'm taking my sister's place. I'm taking notes for her and presenting the paper she wrote."

"She's ill?" The lines around his mouth creased in concern, which made him seem a bit more human.

"Not exactly. She's expecting a baby. Minor complications, thank goodness, but she can't travel anymore."

"Are you a Darcy fanatic too, like most Austen fans?" He arched one eyebrow.

"Fanatic? Hardly." I had to stop myself from rolling my eyes. "But my sister is a true believer." I raised my cup to my lips and took a sip. "You?"

"Darcy's not my type." His expression was so impassive that I couldn't tell whether he was joking or serious. "But Jane Austen books are selling so well—we can't afford to ignore them."

"So you're hoping to develop a sudden affection for all things Austen and make a fortune off of it?"

"At least an understanding of her appeal." He swirled the tea in his cup as if considering whether it was worth his while to drink any more of it.

As suddenly as James had appeared in the doorway, another figure materialized next to my chair.

"Ms. Prescott?" The young woman from the registration desk. "There you are. Your luggage has been taken to your room, if you'd like to unpack."

"Thank you. I would." Salvation in the form of a perky girl with more holes in her body than anyone really needed. I turned to James. "If you'll excuse me?"

"Of course." He rose when I did. For a rude guy, he could exhibit decent manners when he tried. "I'll see you later."

I nodded and followed the young woman out of the Junior Commons, not sure whether to be relieved or disappointed at my escape. I wasn't used to attracting notice from a man like that, and I certainly wasn't accustomed to having that kind of spine-tingling response to a guy. James Beaufort was way out of my league, but at least the scenery at the seminar was going to be as gorgeous as the Oxfordshire countryside.

A wiser woman would have sensed at that moment that trouble was coming. A more experienced woman would have guarded her secrets—and her heart. Sadly, as I made my way up the four flights of stairs to my room, I was neither wise nor experienced.

By the end of the week I would be.

CHAPTER
TWO

he Great Hall at Christ Church was straight out of a Harry Potter movie. Literally. They'd actually done some filming there. But the dining hall didn't need digital special effects to impress and overwhelm me. I took two steps inside the door and stopped, trying to keep my jaw from hanging open.

Portraits of prime ministers, statesmen, literary giants, and other assorted famous alumni lined the wood-paneled walls. Massive fireplaces punctuated the longer walls, and above the dark paneling, huge expanses of stone supported the high arches and the mullioned windows I'd noticed when I first entered the quad. High above, the ceiling arched like a cathedral, heavily beamed and dotted with gilt ornaments. At the far end of the room, a raised dais, covered with a red carpet, held a long table and substantial chairs.

The long rows of tables in front of me were topped with snowy linen and dotted with small, elegant lamps. If I hadn't been starving, I would have turned tail and run. Instead, I kept breathing, moving forward, until I spotted the elderly man who had been in the Junior Common Room earlier.

"May I join you?" I forced myself to say. I knew from experience that I got along very well with older people. For one thing, I would just as soon listen as talk, and they usually had lots of interesting stories to tell.

"Please do." The man nodded to the seat across from him.

"Thank you." I slid into the chair. "I'm Claire. Claire Prescott."

"Martin Blakely."

I shook his extended hand, careful to offer no more than a slight squeeze to the fingers crumpled from arthritis. "It's nice to meet you."

Martin smiled at me with such kindness that I was able to relax for a moment. "I noticed you in the Common Room this morning," he said. "Which seminar are you enrolled in?"

"*Pride and Prejudice*. What about you?"

"The same." He nodded with approval. "We'll be classmates, then."

Thank goodness. I needed for the Jane Austen seminar to be full of safe elderly people like Martin, not arrogant, handsome distractions like James Beaufort.

"I'm afraid I'll be the slowest one in the class," I said in the lightest tone I could manage. "I'm new to Jane Austen."

Martin nodded soberly, but there was a twinkle in his eye. "So you're not hopelessly in love with Mr. Darcy yet?"

I shook my head a little too emphatically. "No. That would be my sister, not me." But even as I said the words, I was aware of forcing the smile on my face. "Besides, I think my boyfriend might object."

Boyfriend is an odd word, really, for describing the romantic partner of a woman over thirty years of age, but that's what Neil was. With the emphasis, I sometimes thought, on the *boy* half of the equation.

"He let you out of the country without him?" Martin shook his head and made a *tut-tutting* kind of noise, but I could tell he was teasing me.

"To tell the truth, I'm not sure he'll notice that I've left. It's baseball season." I tried to maintain that same light tone, but now the strain in my voice was obvious.

"A sports nut, is he?" Martin eyed me thoughtfully, and I tried not to squirm.

"We're pretty casual, actually," I said and took a big gulp from the crystal goblet in front of me. "It's no big deal."

How on earth had the conversation taken such a serious turn?

Martin reached across the table and patted my hand where it rested next to the goblet I'd just drained. "If he comes to his senses, Claire, then he's the right one for you. If not..." He trailed off, looking around the room. "Well, if not, perhaps you might find your own Mr. Darcy right here in Oxford."

I frowned. "I don't see the appeal. He's rude, arrogant, and unpleasant most of the time. My sister thinks he's the ultimate romantic hero, but I just don't get it."

I broke off as a shadow loomed at my right hand. I looked up, and there was my nemesis himself.

"May I?" James nodded at the chair next to me.

"Sure," I said, although I wasn't sure at all. In fact, I would have preferred him to choose a seat at the opposite end of the massive dining hall. The mere fact of his presence had sent my pulse racing again, and my stomach twisted until I was sure I'd never have room for even the first bite of my meal.

Reluctantly I introduced him to Martin, and James took his seat beside me. The nerves on the right side of my body stood at attention, alert to his every movement. That sensitivity left me with a clenched jaw and very little to say for myself. I had never been so aware of another human being. Why did it have to be someone I didn't even particularly like?

Shortly after that, the meal was served. Literally served by waiters. I'd never imagined anything like that in a college refectory. The handful of times I'd been to visit Missy at the University of Missouri, we'd eaten from the salad bar in her dorm's dining hall. Now I was being served food that looked like a photograph from a cooking magazine, in the most exquisite setting I could ever have imagined.

"You didn't tell me," James said to me, "what you do for a living."

I choked on the entrée and coughed for several long

moments. The blood rushed to my face, not because of physical distress, but out of pure embarrassment. What was I supposed to say in front of all of these well-educated, successful people? Certainly not the truth.

Instead, I blurted out an answer that took me by surprise. "I'm a pediatrician." The words slipped out easy as pie, to my great shame.

"So it's Dr. Prescott?" James said, his expression half disbelief, and I bristled.

"Yes." I resisted the urge to offer some explanation that would only make me sound like the liar I was.

"My son is an internist," Martin said with a disapproving glance at James. "A *single* internist," he added with another of his smiles. "Maybe—"

"What made you go into pediatrics?" James interrupted Martin's matchmaking.

"I guess I just love children." It was a lame, bad beauty-pageant answer, but somehow when this man was near me, my IQ dropped a good twenty points.

Martin nodded with approval, James gave me another assessing look, and I changed the subject before either of them could ask another question about my faux career.

"Have you been walking along the river yet?" I asked Martin. "I can see part of it from my window, but I haven't ventured out." I refused to be intimidated by either Oxford or James Beaufort. Well, okay, perhaps *refused* wasn't quite the right word. Both the setting and the company intimidated me.

"I arrived a few days early," Martin said. "To do a bit of exploring." He winked at me. "Or uncover a few secrets."

James frowned, and I returned Martin's smile. "That gives me something to look forward to, then. Where are the best places to uncover some of these secrets?"

Martin paused, wiped his mouth with his napkin, and then gave me a thoughtful look. "Well, along the river, certainly. And perhaps the Botanic Garden. Very beautiful and relaxing. And Blackwell's bookstore, of course . . ."

"I'll put them all on my list," I said. One waiter appeared to remove our plates, and another set dessert in front of us— some sort of combination of cake and custard that promised to be a mother lode of sugar and fat. I sighed with pleasure.

James gave me an austere look, but Martin picked up his spoon and nodded his approval. "All manner of sweet sins fall under the category of 'pudding.' It's one of my favorite things about England."

After a few bites, I had to agree. Martin's easy conversation, the excellent food, and the extraordinary atmosphere lulled me into a sense of peace that I hadn't recovered since my boss called me into his office two weeks before and informed me that my services were no longer required. Apparently it was much more cost-efficient to replace me, a seasoned office manager, with a twenty-two-year-old who had just graduated from college. I took another bite of the "pudding" and pushed away thoughts of home.

✤✤✤✤✤

With a little effort and a few verbal spins, I kept the conversation focused on Oxford and the upcoming seminar. James didn't ask me any more questions about myself, but the die had been cast, and now I was stuck with the untruths and half-truths that my own inadequacy had called forth. As soon as I could, I excused myself and headed to the solace—and protection—of my dorm.

My room was tucked away at the top of four steep flights in a Victorian addition to the college close to the river. I locked the door behind me and plopped onto the bed, as close to the open window and any hope of a fresh breeze as possible. Then I fumbled in my purse for my cell phone.

I had at least found time in the midst of my last-minute packing frenzy to call my cell-phone provider and have the international service turned on. Yes, the cost was in excess of a dollar a minute, but at that moment, I would gladly have parted with a lot more of my shrinking bank balance to hear my sister's voice on the other end of the line.

The phone rang so many times, I was sure she wasn't going to answer. I knew she was home—after all, it was the middle of the day back in Kansas City. Finally, just before the machine could kick in, I heard a rustle, then a thud, and finally the frantic voice of my sister.

"Claire? Are you okay?" I could hear my nieces shrieking in the background and the television blaring. "I thought you weren't going to call unless there was an emergency."

I cringed at the note of alarm in her voice. "I'm fine,

I'm fine. Don't panic." I hadn't meant to scare her. "I just called . . ." Why had I called? I didn't have a reason, really. Not a practical one anyway. "Just wanted to call and say that I got here okay."

"Oh. Okay. That's great."

I didn't know what else to say, but I was reluctant to break the connection. Missy was everything that was familiar and comfortable, and at that moment I needed some bit of home to steady me.

"Was there something else?" Missy said in a distracted voice. "I promised the girls I'd take them to the pool."

"I'm sorry." I pressed the phone closer to my ear, as if by doing so I could bring her closer to me. "I guess I just needed to hear a friendly voice."

"There are unfriendly voices? At Christ Church? I thought they ate tourists up with a spoon. All those lovely American dollars flowing into their accounts."

"No one's been unfriendly," I said to reassure her. "It's just that . . ." What? It was just that what? "I guess I'm just a little homesick," I said with what I hoped was a convincing amount of ruefulness.

"But you just got there," Missy said with a laugh. "Give it some time. You'll feel better after a good night's sleep."

"I know. I'm sorry. I'm okay, really. You feeling okay?" I much preferred the familiar role of soothing older sister.

"I'm fine. Quit worrying."

"What about Phillip's dry cleaning? Did you remember to pick it up?" Before I left I had made Missy a list of everything I usually did for her, but even though I'd written it all down, I wasn't sure she'd remember.

"Yes, Claire. I got the dry cleaning. And remembered to give the dog his heartworm pill. Now relax and enjoy Oxford. Don't worry about us."

"Okay. I will. Take care." I was just about to pull the phone away from my ear and hit the red button to disconnect the call when Missy's voice stopped me.

"Claire," she asked in a soft voice, "why did you really call?"

Her question caught me off guard. I'd been sitting on the bed, but suddenly I was so tired I had to lie down. I eased my head to the pillow and sank gratefully into the mattress, the phone still pressed to my ear.

"I'm scared." I couldn't believe I'd said it aloud, especially not to Missy. In all the years since our parents had died, I'd never admitted to fear. I couldn't afford to admit to it. I couldn't have risked it, not when I had to stay strong for Missy. But now Missy was safe and I was overwhelmed, and suddenly it was all too much.

"Oh, sis." I could hear the tears in Missy's voice. "What's scaring you?"

I wished I'd thought to pack tissues. I wiped at my eyes with the back of my free hand.

"I met someone," I whispered. "I met someone who scares me, and that's never happened before."

Silence. A long, stunned silence, followed by a heavy weight pressed against my chest.

"I assume you mean in a romantic man-woman kind of way," Missy said at last. "Not in a scary stalker-guy kind of way."

Romantic? I hadn't thought of my reaction to James that way. Electric? Yes. Terrifying? Absolutely. But romantic?

"Yes. I guess so. I mean...I don't know, Missy. I don't know what I mean."

She was quiet for a long moment. "What about Neil?"

That was the question I'd been dreading, the one I'd been avoiding asking myself.

"It's not like I'm embarking on some clandestine affair. I don't think this guy even likes me."

"Well, he's a fool if he doesn't."

I snorted with laughter. "Thanks for the sisterly vote of confidence, but I'm just being realistic. He's gorgeous, he looks rich, and he's from some old New York publishing family. Definitely out of my league."

"League? Out of your league?" Missy made a fussing noise. "Did he say—"

"No, of course he didn't." I switched my cell phone to my other ear. I wanted to say, "He didn't have to," but I refrained. No point in getting Missy as worked up as I was. "He was a perfect gentleman." Which was technically true.

"Hmm." Missy sounded unconvinced.

"Really. I'll be okay. I don't know why I'm being so dramatic. It's probably just the jet lag." It had been a mistake to call home. I felt worse now than I had five minutes before. "I'll call you again on Monday after the first session. Let you know what you're missing."

"You sure?"

"Absolutely." But I paused for a moment, aware that once I pushed the red button to end the call, I'd be on my own once again.

"Try to have a good time," Missy said, sounding like the older sister instead of the younger one. "We'll sort everything else out when you get home."

I knew she meant well, but it didn't help to be reminded that in addition to losing my job, I'd lost some of my cachet as the competent, successful older sister. My new circumstances had leveled the playing field for Missy and me.

"I know. Thanks. I'm sorry to keep you."

"You know you can call anytime."

"I know." Tears sprang to my eyes. How many times had I said that exact same thing to Missy? It was the first time, however, that she'd ever said it to me.

"Bye," I whispered.

"Bye."

She hung up first, which shouldn't have bothered me, but it did. I clutched the phone in my hand and did what I had wanted to do all day. I cried from exhaustion, from confusion, even from remorse. I cried in a way that I hadn't cried since my parents' death. There was no one to hear me, just the faint sounds of other participants making their way to their rooms, and the last calls of the birds in the dying light of evening as they made their way home over the delicate, dreaming spires of Oxford.

ortunately for me, the seminar didn't begin until Monday. Instead we were allowed a true Sabbath, a Sunday of rest to get over our jet lag and prepare for the coming week. I slept late, a combination of the time difference and my emotional and physical exhaustion. Consequently I missed breakfast in the Hall and resorted to a protein bar and a cup of tea brewed in my room.

By late morning, I was ready to face the world, but I wasn't looking forward to meeting James Beaufort and the other perfectly nice people whom I'd lied to so easily. Rather than encounter any of them, I grabbed my copy of *Pride and Prejudice* and slipped out the side gate of the Meadow Building. I crossed the broad gravel walk that separated the college from Christ Church Meadow and turned beneath the canopy of trees down a second path known as the King's Walk.

Here the trees arched above me like the ceiling of the Hall, only greener. I was grateful for the shelter from the blazing sun. The gravel crunched beneath my sandals as I walked. The air was less oppressive in the shade but still warm. I was headed toward the river about a hundred yards away. Maybe I could find a nice quiet spot and review the book before the seminar began the next day. A few people moved up and down the path in a desultory fashion. I raised my gaze to the branches so far above my head, as different from the hardy Midwestern foliage at home as anything could be. Here was God's majesty, here was grandeur, here was—

"Hello."

The voice startled me, and I stumbled over my own feet. I regained my balance, and my gaze swung to the elderly woman sitting on a bench a few feet off the path. Only it wasn't a bench at all but a large tree stump. Her short cap of salt-and-pepper hair looked as if she hadn't washed it in a while, and in spite of the heat, she was wrapped in a teal trench coat. Her eyes, blue and intense, burned in her weathered face.

I didn't know what to say, so I simply stared at her for a long moment before I collected both my wits and the good manners my mother had drilled into me as a child.

"Hello." I tried not to sound as wary as I felt.

"Would you care to buy some cards?" She held out a handful of heavy yellowed paper.

I froze. Only figuratively, of course, given the heat. "I, um—"

"No need to poker up, my dear. I'm not a beggar or a luna-
tic. Merely an old woman on a pension."

My cheeks flushed. "I didn't mean—"

"No, of course not." Laugh lines made deep creases at the
corners of her eyes. She shifted to one side of the oversized
stump and patted the spot next to her. "Do have a seat."

I had no idea why I was afraid of this wrinkled gnome of a
lady, but I hesitated.

"Is that Jane Austen you're reading?" She nodded toward
the book in my hand. "She's a favorite of mine. Please, do sit
down."

What could I do? "Thank you." I forced myself to say the
words and wade through the knee-high grass and wildflowers
surrounding her perch. I sat down beside her. She smelled of
talcum powder and must and perhaps just a hint of sherry.

"You're staying at the college?" She nodded in the direction of Christ Church.

"Yes. I'm here for a seminar." I indicated the book in my
hand. "On this."

"Ah." She nodded as if I'd just said something very wise.
"You'll be presenting a paper, then." She had a strange sparkle
in her eye.

"Yes." I decided to forgo explaining that it was Missy's
paper, not mine. "The seminar's on *Pride and Prejudice*."

"Mr. Darcy, is it?" She smiled. "And which version of that
gentleman do you subscribe to?" She paused, and her eyes

grew hazy. "In my day, we swooned over Olivier in the role, although they murdered the novel in that one." She looked at me, her gaze back in focus. "I suppose you fancy that Colin Firth? Or the newer one. That morose-looking chap." She continued without waiting for me to answer. "No two are quite the same, of course. Not even in the—"

She stopped and clamped her lips together. "No. I mustn't. But…" She leaned toward me, and her bright blue gaze pierced mine. "Are you happy?"

The abrupt change of subject threw me for a moment. "Happy?" I echoed. She was watching for my reaction so closely that I felt like the proverbial bug under a microscope.

"You look very sad." She lifted her hand and rested it atop mine.

To my surprise, I didn't pull away from her touch. Tears stung my eyes. I'd always hidden my emotions well. It must have been the jet lag. Or the strangeness of finding myself in such an alien world.

"Why would you say I look sad?" I swiped the tears away from my eyes.

She chuckled and curled her gnarled fingers around mine. "I'm called Harriet. Harriet Dalrymple."

I lightly returned the pressure of her fingers. "Claire Prescott. It's nice to meet you."

"Is it?" She laughed. "I'm surprised you think so. Most of the summer people from the college avoid me like the plague. Especially the Americans."

"I'm sure——" But I stopped, not really sure of anything anymore.

"So, it's Mr. Darcy, is it?" She nodded toward the book I was holding.

"Yes." And my fear returned. I inched away from her on the stump. "Academically speaking, of course. Not personally. As a romantic icon, I think he's overrated."

"Of course."

"It's not like I'm personally obsessed with him." I could hear the defensiveness in my voice.

"Of course not." She released my hand. "You know, I happen to be a distant cousin of the Austens," she said as casually as if we were discussing the weather. "I even have some of her old papers."

I studied her expression, prickles of suspicion darting up my spine. I was pretty sure she was either lying or crazy. Most likely just a garden-variety cat lady suffering the beginnings of dementia.

"Her uncle was a Master here, you know," she said, waving a hand in the direction of the city behind us. "Not at Christ Church. Balliol College. She was even sent to school here for a time when she was a girl."

I vaguely remembered reading those details about Austen's life in the introduction to my copy of *Pride and Prejudice*. "And you're related to her——"

"Through the uncle. The papers were passed down through that branch of the family."

They were probably nothing, of course, those papers. Grocery lists. Or forgeries. Wishful family thinking.

"You haven't told me your name," the woman said, interrupting my thoughts. "I'm Harriet. Harriet Dalrymple."

My heart sank. She didn't remember that we'd introduced ourselves only moments ago. Clearly her mental faculties were on the decline. All her talk of being related to Jane Austen was obviously a delusion.

"Mrs. Dalrymple—"

"Harriet, please."

"It's awfully warm here, even in the shade. Wouldn't you be more comfortable at home?" I wondered if there was anyone there, waiting for her, or someone who might be looking for her. I wouldn't have been surprised to find that she'd wandered away from a nursing home or some kind of assisted-living facility.

Harriet glanced around as if she were only just then noticing her surroundings. "Oh yes. I suppose so. Do you think I should go home?" She looked down at the cards in her lap. I could see now that they were pen-and-ink renderings. Quite good ones, really. I recognized Tom Tower and the tree-lined King's Walk where we were sitting. "I haven't sold my cards," she said in a sad voice.

"I'll buy them." I had no idea what they cost, but I couldn't let her continue to sit there in the heat in that trench coat. In fact, I thought I should help her find her way home before she became so disoriented that she didn't remember where she lived.

"You'll buy my cards?"

I nodded. "And I'd like to walk you home too, if you don't mind."

She smiled, and her tanned and wrinkled face looked much younger. "That would be lovely. We can have a cup of tea."

"Of course we can," I said, even as the thought of another hot beverage caused fresh perspiration to bead on my forehead.

I helped her to her feet, and we waded through the grass to the path. I paused, waiting for her to indicate which direction we should go, but she merely looked around as if she were seeing the scene for the first time.

"Is your home in that direction?" I waved toward the college. "Or should we go the other way? Along the river?"

Harriet didn't answer for a long moment. Long enough for me to wonder how I would go about finding a policeman who could help me find her place of residence.

And then she came to, so to speak. Awakened from whatever twilight sleep had gripped her. She took my arm and turned me toward the river.

"This way, Miss Prescott. Do you prefer cake or muffin?"

"Um—"

"Or perhaps a bit of both? Why not?" she said with a chuckle. "After all, it's not every day that I make a new friend from America."

❧❧❧❧❧❧

I'd never been in a real English cottage before. For years I'd collected them, though. Missy gave me one each year for my birthday. Little figurines by David Winter that were all thatched roofs, dark beams and plaster, climbing roses and trailing vines.

Harriet Dalrymple's home embodied all of the things I loved about those miniature houses. It sat back from the river, a bit apart from the other cottages nearby, and the front garden bloomed scarlet, yellow, and lavender amid the lush greenery. A stone path led to the front door, and I had to duck so I wouldn't hit my head on the lintel. The entrance led to a narrow passageway crammed with bric-a-brac and books, the odd mirror dotting the fading wallpaper.

"Go on through to the sitting room, dear," she said as she unbelted her trench coat and hung it on a peg by the door. "I'll make some tea."

Inside the cottage, the air was still, but not suffocating. The thick walls must have kept out the summer heat. I followed the direction she'd indicated with a wave of her hand and ducked through yet another doorway.

The sitting room looked like a cross between a Beatrix Potter illustration and Miss Havisham's house in *Great Expectations*. Charming but dusty, with several cobwebs stringing from the ceiling to the tops of the bookshelves and then to the large armoire in the corner. An overstuffed sofa and chairs covered with fading pink cabbage roses filled the room almost to bursting, and more books were stacked along the open stretches of baseboard.

I slowly circled the room, taking in the minutiae of the older woman's life. A drinks cabinet held a few bottles of sherry and some spotted glassware. A calendar of the Lake District, circa 1988, hung above the writing desk in the far corner.

"It's like a museum," I murmured to myself.

"It is, isn't it?"

I jumped at the sound of her voice, and then I blushed. "I'm sorry—"

"No need to apologize for telling the truth, dear. Besides, that's quite the effect I was going for. The past is such a comforting place. Far less distressing than the present."

Given my personal history, I couldn't agree with her on that score, so I changed the subject. "All these books…" I nodded toward the stacks along one wall. "Were you a professor?"

She laughed at my question, a sound that was both dry and watery at the same time.

"Women weren't given that chance in my day."

I waited for her to expound on her answer. Instead, she waved me toward the sofa. "Sit down. The tea will be ready in a moment. Lovely things, electric kettles. Although"—she paused as she settled into a chair beneath the front window that overlooked her garden and the lane beyond—"there's something to be said for taking one's time. No one seems to have much of a taste for that these days."

"No, I don't guess they do." I knew that I didn't. My life was a constant whirl of activity. Or at least it had been until I was fired. Now I had more leisure at my disposal than even my newfound friend might have wished for.

"You mentioned you had some of Jane Austen's papers. Would you consider showing them to me?" I asked. I would look at them and find some way to gently explain that they weren't real. I hated to see her persist with this delusion that she owned some undiscovered treasure of one of the greatest writers in the English language.

"Oh." She looked at me with consideration, as if she were sizing me up. "I suppose it wouldn't do any harm to just share a bit..." She leaned forward in the chair and bit her lip as her gaze scanned the room. "Ah yes. Now I remember."

"It's Austen's first draft of *Pride and Prejudice*, you know." She hoisted herself from the sagging cushion and crossed to the drinks cabinet. "I was rereading it last night with a glass of port."

Well, of course she had been. I sighed. What else could I do but play along? Clearly she was delusional.

"I'm surprised you keep something that valuable at your house. Shouldn't you donate it to a museum or something?"

Harriet chuckled. "Dear, as you said yourself, my house is a museum."

I couldn't argue with that.

"Here we are." She pulled a sheaf of yellowed paper from a shelf above the cabinet and then crossed to the sofa. She placed the stack of paper in my hands. "Why don't you get started while I get the tea?"

I'd come to her cottage half out of pity, half out of curiosity, but the moment she placed that crumbling manuscript in my hands, an unexplained shiver ran over my body. I glanced down and lowered it to my lap. Harriet bustled off to the kitchen, and I was left with a pile of paper that looked very old indeed. Old enough to actually be—

No, that was ridiculous. She'd probably written it herself. A flight of fancy, although that did seem to be Harriet's normal state rather than a departure. At that moment, though, fancy appealed to me far more than reality did.

I looked down and began to read.

First Impressions

Chapter One

It is a truth universally acknowledged that a single man in possession of a good fortune must be in want of a wife. Therefore when a gentleman by the name of Bingley inquired as to letting the great house at Netherfield, the village of Meryton and its environs blossomed with expectation, for it had been many years since so interesting a development had occurred in that part of Hertfordshire.

y head shot up, and I looked around for Harriet, but she was still in the kitchen. I could hear her talking to herself, and then she chuckled. I glanced down at the pages in my lap again. The handwriting was old-fashioned but neat, the

ink faded to a soft brown. The wording was similar, true, to the beginning of *Pride and Prejudice*, but fan fiction might have existed back in the early nineteenth century just as it did now. Could it be the real thing? I continued reading.

> *Mrs. Long reported to all who were interested, and to some who were not, that Mr. Bingley had five thousand a year, two sisters, and no wife. If the amount of his fortune proved true, the young women of the village agreed they might forgive him the sisters—provided they were allowed to furnish him with the wife.*
>
> *But, alas, upon finding that the Bennets, a principal family of the neighborhood, had recently entered into a year of mourning at the death of their husband and father, the enticing Mr. Bingley set aside his designs on Hertfordshire and settled his affections on Derbyshire instead.*

Death of Mr. Bennet? This wasn't *Pride and Prejudice*. Mr. Bennet didn't die in the real book. And how could Mr. Bingley wind up married to Jane if he never moved to their neighborhood?

> *The young ladies of Meryton were not doomed to disappointment forever, although the addition of another gentleman to the neighborhood came at a dear price indeed. Upon the death of Mr. Bennet, the Rev. Mr. Collins, an estranged cousin of the family, inherited the estate of Longbourn. The late Mr. Bennet had resided at the manor*

for enough years to leave behind a widow and five grown but unmarried daughters.

Mr. Collins, devoted clergyman that he was, quickly perceived upon arriving for his cousin's funeral that his duty was to serve as trusted advisor to the widowed Mrs. Bennet. He promised to return to Longbourn within a fortnight to assist the young ladies in overcoming their grief and Mrs. Bennet in securing a new situation, for he was eager to take possession of the house and forsake his clerical duties for the life of a gentleman.

Again, the plot was all wrong. Mr. Collins ended up marrying Elizabeth's friend Miss Lucas, but they lived in his parsonage. In the real book, he proposed to Elizabeth, who turned him down, much to her mother's distress.

Mrs. Bennet, however, took a great deal longer than a mere fortnight to recover from the cruel blow of her husband's demise. She sent letters to the parsonage at Huntsford every se'ennight, begging Mr. Collins would delay his return to Longbourn a little longer. This tactic, rendered more effective by the teardrops Mrs. Bennet allowed to fall upon the paper as she wrote, permitted the widow and her daughters to persist in their home for a full half of their required year of mourning.

That sounded more like the real book, but it still wasn't right. Mr. Collins didn't kick the Bennets out of their house in the novel. I flipped through the pages in my lap. What Harriet had given me was a small section of a larger piece, and it was clearly a working draft. The margins contained notes in the same handwriting, and here and there words had been scribbled out and replaced.

Still, the time came when the inevitable could no longer be delayed.

"We must remove from Longbourn, Mama," said Elizabeth after breakfast one day as she studied the contents of Mr. Collins' latest missive. She was alone with her mother in the morning room. "Our cousin is eager to take his place in our local society, and we have imposed on his forbearance long enough."

Mrs. Bennet sniffed, rose from her chair at the little desk, and frowned at her second eldest daughter.

"Forbearance? He is a clergyman. Certainly the practice requires no effort on his part, for he must be accustomed to it." She pushed aside the household account book Elizabeth had pressed upon her. "Why Mr. Collins insists on having Longbourn when he enjoys a perfectly adequate parsonage at Huntsford, I am sure I do not know. A manor requires such upkeep, and it is all quite worrying. Surely he wishes to be spared the turmoil that caused your father's untimely...untimely...." She could not continue, but instead sank onto the settee and covered her face with her handkerchief as she began to weep once more.

Well, that certainly sounded like the Mrs. Bennet from the real novel.

Elizabeth sighed and pulled the account book toward her. She had long given up any private embarrassment at her mother's behavior. Public humiliation, however, was not so easily avoided. She opened the book and eyed the most recent column of figures. If only she could magically transpose the numbers there into an order that would relieve her mind rather than trouble it. Such conjuring was beyond her powers, however, and wishful thinking would not change their situation. The Bennet family sank further into debt each day.

"We might remove to the seaside," Elizabeth said to her mother, though the woman's face was still obscured by her handkerchief.

At the mention of the seaside, her sobs quieted a little.

"You have always wished for some sea bathing to calm your nerves." Elizabeth was on intimate terms with her mother's nerves. Like her father before her, she had heard them mentioned with consideration for many years. The reminder of Mr. Bennet, and the rent his demise had left in the family fabric, caused a lump to rise in Elizabeth's throat. After half a year she expected to feel his loss less keenly, yet it was not so. She grieved his death as much

now as the day he'd been laid to rest in the churchyard at
Meryton.

"The seaside?" Mrs. Bennet echoed, lowering the
handkerchief. "A little cottage might do, I suppose. Ten
rooms, I should think."

Elizabeth sighed and closed the account book. Her
mother might as well wish for a hundred rooms as ten.

"We must entertain more modest expectations, Mama.
If we are frugal, we may manage three or four."

Elizabeth knew what must happen once her mother and
sisters were settled in their new home. To secure her future,
a gentlewoman must either marry or seek employment.

Jane, her elder sister, could reasonably be expected to
procure a husband through the twin inducements of her
beauty and pleasant nature. Indeed, Elizabeth had already
arranged with her aunt and uncle Gardiner, who resided in
London, for Jane to travel to town once the rest of the family
had found a situation. If Jane could but make herself
known in a wider society, a proposal must soon follow.

Elizabeth's own chances of entertaining an offer of
marriage were much less encouraging. She had neither
Jane's beauty nor goodness, and she was far too likely to
say what she thought. Her frankness had sent potential
suitors scurrying on more than one occasion. Combined with
her lack of dowry—well, Elizabeth had no faith in fairy
stories. Her future must be the work of her own hands.

I paused in my reading. This alternate version certainly seemed connected to the real one, but how could such a manuscript have survived all these years without being discovered by the world?

"I still do not comprehend how we may be thrown into the street, merely because of an entail."

Mrs. Bennet's oft-used lament strained the last of Elizabeth's patience. She had tried in vain, as had her father before her, to explain the terms on which her father had come by Longbourn. Since the manor was entailed, only the nearest male relative could inherit the property. Despite many lengthy explanations, however, her mother refused to acknowledge Mr. Collins' legal right to avail himself of the roof and walls, much less the very furnishings and plate, that she had enjoyed throughout her married life.

"We are not to be thrown into the street, Mama," Elizabeth said as kindly as she could. "Mr. Collins is a gentleman, not a bill collector."

A soft rap on the door relieved Elizabeth of the endless duty of placating her mother.

"Yes?"

Hill, the housekeeper, opened the door and peered around it. "The ladies have a visitor," she said.

Elizabeth clutched the account book tightly. She had hoped to avoid tradesmen appearing at the house demanding payment, but even the kindest merchants in Meryton had begun to inquire as to when the Misses Bennet might cross their palms with a bit of silver.

To her shock, however, the door opened fully to reveal their cousin, Mr. Collins himself, standing on the threshold.

"Mr. Collins! You are come," Elizabeth blurted out.

The Rev. Mr. Collins failed to register the dismay in her tone. He smiled, sketched a bow, and entered the room. "Miss Elizabeth. Mrs. Bennet. You are in good health, I trust?" He did not pause for an answer but continued, "I bring you the compliments of my most esteemed patroness, Lady Catherine de Bourgh, who urged me to delay my return to Longbourn no longer."

Having spent several days in her cousin's tedious company, Elizabeth could well imagine that the gentleman's patroness had been glad to encourage him on his way.

"We are delighted to see you, Mr. Collins. I trust you are in good health as well." Elizabeth rose and made her curtsy since her mother showed no signs of greeting the new master of Longbourn in a proper manner.

"Mr. Collins," her mother said from where she reclined on the settee. "How good of you to come to minister to us in our grief."

The gentleman's brow creased for a moment at this manner of address, for he had expected to find Mrs. Bennet quite recovered from her husband's death. Instead, she showed no more sign of relinquishing her hold upon the *house than she had six months before, greeting him as a visitor rather than the master. Elizabeth stifled a sigh. Six years, much less six months, would not be sufficient to persuade her mother that Longbourn was no longer theirs.*

"I am at your service, madam," Mr. Collins said with yet another bow. His manners were all civility, yet he could not help but cast an assessing eye over the room. "Your sisters are also well, I trust?" he asked Elizabeth when she seated herself again in her chair and motioned for him to occupy the one opposite.

"Yes, thank you. Jane prepares to travel to London to stay with my aunt and uncle Gardiner."

His face sagged in disappointment, which only confirmed to Elizabeth the necessity of her decision. She had not misread Mr. Collins' pointed attentions to Jane at their father's funeral. "And your other sisters? Where shall they be sent?"

Mr. Collins' easy assumption that the family would be so quickly dissolved irritated Elizabeth, but she kept her tone civil. "My other sisters shall accompany Mama once a proper situation has been procured."

"And yourself?"

"My plans are uncertain as yet."

"Indeed." He inclined his head and eyed her with speculation. Elizabeth looked away.

"Uncertain?" Mrs. Bennet interrupted. "Why should your plans be uncertain, Lizzie? I'm sure you have spoken of nothing but the seaside since breakfast."

Elizabeth had meant to broach the subject of her own future with her mother once Mrs. Bennet had grasped the contents of the household account book and therefore the gravity of their situation, but she could delay the truth no longer.

"I mean to seek employment, Mama."

arriet entered the room with the tea tray, and I reluctantly set aside the unread portion of the manuscript.

"Do you prefer lemon or milk?" she asked as she set the tray on a low table between the sofa and the chair beneath the window. She sank into the chair and then righted herself so that she could perch on the edge and pour out the tea.

"Milk, please."

"Sugar?"

"Yes."

The perfectly normal conversation felt completely at odds with the situation and the pages on the sofa next to me. I took my cup from Harriet and declined her offer of a biscuit.

"What do you think so far?" Harriet asked.

"I have no idea what to think." It was the most honest answer I could come up with.

Harriet smiled. "I understand." She glanced at the unread pages next to me. "Please, don't mind me."

What else could I do but resume reading? I took a sip of tea and then returned to the task at hand.

Jane and Elizabeth slipped unnoticed into the garden, and beyond it to the little wood where they so often withdrew for sisterly consolation.

"What shall I do without you, Jane?" Elizabeth asked as they strolled along the path, arm in arm. "You are the only thing that prevents me from becoming the veriest harpy."

"I should not go," Jane said, her lips drawn and her voice sober. "'Tis not fair to leave you to manage so much. I am the eldest."

"And the most likely to make a brilliant match and save us all from poverty," Elizabeth said with a teasing smile.

Jane sighed. "I would not wager my pin money upon it. I daresay London gentlemen will find me a country drab."

Elizabeth stopped in the middle of the path and pulled her sister around to face her. "Any London gentleman, even one of the meanest understanding, could not fail to appreciate you, Jane. And if one fails to do so—"

"What? What shall you do?" Jane teased. "Call him out? Challenge him to a duel? What a scandal that would be."

Both sisters grew quiet for a moment. The carefree days of the past were buried as surely as Mr. Bennet was interred in the churchyard at Meryton.

Jane took her sister's hands. "I should be the one to go with Mama. You should go to London, Elizabeth, for you would not be afraid to enter into society."

"I should offend that very society within a se'ennight and be sent packing," Elizabeth replied with a laugh.

Jane could not deny the truth of that statement and so only smiled. Elizabeth turned back the way they had come, leading Jane along behind her.

"No, Jane, you must go to London and make a brilliant match. Then, when your wealthy husband buys you a town house in Mayfair, we shall all come to live with you, which will force your generous husband to flee to the country, leaving us all a happy family party once more."

Jane chuckled as Elizabeth had intended. "Lizzie, once Mama is settled with our sisters, you must come to London for a visit as well, even if it is a short one." Elizabeth made a noise as if to protest, but Jane would not allow it. "No, Lizzie. I won't stand for argument on that score." Her eyes grew misty. "You have been the very mortar that has held Longbourn in one piece since Papa's death. You deserve your share of amusement more than any of us."

"Then I shall brook no less than a formal presentation at court," Elizabeth teased, but despite the lightness she forced into her tone, she was far from sanguine.

Jane put an arm around her shoulders. "If I could, I would buy your presentation clothes myself."

If only one of them had been born a son. If only her father had implemented a plan of economy twenty years before and put aside something for his wife and children. But with each expectation of a happy event, economy had been delayed in the certainty that this child, at last, would be the longed-for heir. And so instead of living out their days at Longbourn, Mrs. Bennet and her three youngest daughters would be forced to reside in some narrow dockside set of rooms. Jane would be dependent upon the goodwill of her mother's relations and the vagaries of the London marriage mart. And Elizabeth, with few worldly possessions beyond her own pride, would make her living by bowing and scraping before people who were her equals in birth and breeding.

"We shall come about," Elizabeth said to Jane as they entered the house. "Certainly, we shall."

But both sisters felt the emptiness of the words. With heavy hearts, they went to dress for dinner, for surely, now that Mr. Collins had come, this would be among their last meals at Longbourn.

I sat stunned, the yellowed pages of the manuscript scattered across my lap. Surely this couldn't be the real thing. And yet it had a certain quality that seemed so close to the original.

"Would you like more tea, dear?"

She was still there, of course, sitting quietly in the sagging chair beneath the window.

"Um, sure. Yes. Thanks." If only Missy were here. She might know whether this was the real thing. I didn't know enough about Austen to guess. It sure sounded like her work to me. But was it her handwriting? I had no way of knowing. I was the wrong person, the worst person possible, really, to be sitting here trying to decide if this pile of pages was for real. "Have you ever tried to have it authenticated?"

She shook her head. "There's no need, dear."

I nodded. If she chose to use a bogus Austen manuscript to try and befriend people... Well, she was obviously a lonely old woman. I couldn't blame her. I'd probably be just like her someday, luring unsuspecting strangers into my home with the promise of literary secrets and sweets.

"Thank you for letting me read it." I gathered the manuscript pages into a tidy pile, careful not to damage the fragile paper, and handed them to her across the tea table. "It does almost seem as if Jane Austen could have written it."

"She did write it."

I met her bright blue gaze again. Only this time there was nothing bleary or elderly about the way she looked at me.

"How do you know?" Now she was starting to creep me out. And then a sinking feeling lodged in the pit of my stomach. I knew nothing about this woman. I looked at my teacup, afraid I might find some foreign substance swimming in the remains at the bottom.

"There's no need for alarm." She set the manuscript on the table beside the tea things. "It's only that I thought…well, you seem like a nice young woman. I liked you the moment I saw you. I thought perhaps you might help me decide what to do with the manuscript." Harriet looked at me with a plea in her eyes. "I've gotten so muddled in my own mind…"

"It's okay. I won't tell anyone." I paused, wondering what I could say that would best ease her mind. "It can be our little secret."

She shook her head. "No, my dear. Unfortunately, it cannot. Not now that you've seen it."

I leaned down to grab my bag and then rose from the couch. She was a sweet woman, but also a little delusional.

"No one knows I've been here," I said in hopes of humoring her. "Let's just say this afternoon never happened." I glanced at my watch. "Besides, I need to get back. There's a welcome reception at five." I moved toward the doorway and then paused. "Thank you for the tea."

"Wait." Harriet was on her feet in a split second. "I'm afraid I can't let you simply leave."

The hairs on the back of my neck stood at attention. "Can't let me?" I moved into the hallway, but she was hot on my heels. "Good-bye, Mrs. Dalrymple." I practically sprinted for the door.

Again, she was faster than I would have given her credit for.

"Miss Prescott."

I paused, my hand clutching the doorknob in a death grip just as hers pinned my arm. "Yes?"

"This won't be the end of it."

"Really, you don't have to worry." I had the door open and was almost safely outside. "Your secret's safe with me."

She followed me into the small patch of garden that separated her cottage from the road. "I'm afraid you don't understand. The others won't like it that—"

"Good-bye, Mrs. Dalrymple. Thank you again." I took off like a shot down the pavement, afraid that at any moment I'd feel her hand grabbing my arm.

"But, Miss Prescott—"

Even though her distress was clear, I couldn't stop. Enough was enough. I had to get away before I got drawn in any more deeply. Whoever Harriet Dalrymple was and whatever the truth was about that manuscript, I didn't have any business getting involved. Certainly I had problems enough of my own.

I kept moving as quickly as I could, one foot in front of the other, the spires of the colleges in the distance guiding me back to sanity.

o distract myself from the unsettling experience in Harriet Dalrymple's cottage, I decided not to go back to my room at Christ Church but to keep walking until I reached the center of Oxford. I hoped the sight of Sunday-afternoon shoppers might make the world seem normal again. I walked mindlessly, unsure of any destination, until I found myself in front of the famous Blackwell's bookshop on Broad Street. The dark sign with its gilt letters, the flat front with multipaned windows and blue doors, beckoned me inside, and I went seeking the comfort I'd always found in any bookstore I had ever entered.

Blackwell's sprawled over five floors and reminded me more of a library than a store. I made my way through the maze of stacks and let the presence of so many printed words and bound pages reassure me. I needed that stability, that sense of permanence, after what had happened at Harriet's cottage.

Here, in this store, was proof that the older woman's imagination was just that—a comforting flight of fancy but not connected to reality in any way.

I found the fiction section and the A's quite easily, and there they were: volume after volume of Jane Austen's novels in every size, shape, and edition. The slimmer single volumes. Larger compendiums of her collected works. The juvenile writings and the few unfinished novels she'd left behind. Even a thick volume of her collected letters. All known to the world for two hundred years or more. They were real. They were the truth.

I sat down on the wooden bench in the aisle and pulled a leather-bound copy of *Pride and Prejudice* from the shelf, a different edition from the one I already owned, which was now stowed in the bottom of my purse. I reread the first page, mentally comparing the writing with what I'd seen only a few minutes before in Harriet's cottage. I didn't even know who to ask to find out if there was any truth at all to Harriet's assertions, but her belief in the authenticity of the manuscript did trouble me.

"It's a little late to start reading the book now," a voice said from beside me.

I looked up. It was Martin Blakely, clad in a tweed jacket and jaunty cap. He must be part-British, to be able to wear wool in such hot weather.

"Hello, Martin." I couldn't quite get into the spirit of his teasing.

"May I?" He gestured toward the unoccupied end of the bench.

"Sure." I scooted over so he would have enough room.

"I don't mean to intrude, but you seem upset." His bright eyes were friendly but assessing. "Would a listening ear help?"

I shook my head. "No. But I wouldn't mind some friendly conversation."

He reached for the volume of *Pride and Prejudice* that I was holding. "This is lovely. I've not seen this edition before." He examined the book for several moments, flipping through its pages. "Were you planning to buy this one?"

I shook my head. "No."

He turned the book back and forth in his hands. "No matter how much is written about Jane Austen," he said, "she still seems something of a mystery, doesn't she?"

I shrugged. "I'm afraid I don't know enough about her to be a good judge of that."

He paused. "Take this book, for instance. She wrote the first draft of *Pride and Prejudice* before she was twenty-one, you know. I've always found that fascinating."

My heart leaped. "The first draft?" Just when I'd managed to find a measure of calm, Martin's words set me on edge again. "What do you mean, first draft?"

He ran his fingers along the book's spine with a reverent touch. "It was called *First Impressions* then. She finished it in less than two years, if I remember correctly. Her father tried to find a publisher for it but didn't have any luck. I suppose that was fortunate in the end, since she rewrote it a decade or so later. The rewrite's the version we have today."

He lifted the book in his hand for emphasis while I tried not to swallow my tongue. The coincidence was unnerving.

"Wow. You really are an Austen fan," I finally managed to say.

Martin chuckled. "You could say that."

"So have you read this early version? Is it similar?" Even as I asked the question, my chest tightened.

He shook his head. "No copies of it exist. At least, none that are known."

I couldn't help the color that rose to my cheeks. Of course it couldn't be possible, but…

"So *Pride and Prejudice* was her first book?" I asked, eager to distract both him and me.

"No, her second. It came out after *Sense and Sensibility*."

"I can't imagine someone misplacing a manuscript like that. You'd think her family would have wanted it, at least."

Martin leaned forward to rest his hands on his knees. "Her sister Cassandra, who survived her, destroyed a large portion of Jane's letters. I've often wondered whether she might have done the same with *First Impressions*."

My eyes bulged. "She destroyed the work of one of the greatest writers in history?"

"Well, to be fair, she had no way of knowing how her sister's work would be judged two hundred years later."

"I suppose not." Still, the idea boggled the mind.

"The family was very respectable, but they didn't have a lot of money. Reputation was everything, and a gentleman would have been tainted enough by engaging in commerce. A lady would have been condemned for it. All of Austen's books were published anonymously."

I rolled my eyes. "Fortunately times have changed."

"Have they?" Martin shrugged. "I'm not so sure."

Given my recent firing, I thought I might have to agree with him after all.

"I've always wondered—" Martin broke off and looked away.

"What? You've always wondered what?"

He laid his palm flat over the book. "She began *First Impressions* not long after she met a young man named Tom Lefroy. Apparently they engaged in a very public flirtation and were quite taken with each other. But since she had no money, he couldn't seriously consider her as a wife. In fact, his family sent him away before the two of them could do anything foolish."

"You think that her experience had something to do with *Pride and Prejudice*?" I didn't see the connection.

"She began the book only a few months after the Tom Lefroy episode. I'd be surprised if it didn't inspire some of the elements in the novel."

"Such as?" I still didn't understand.

"A young woman of good birth but not much fortune. A young man who must marry to please his family. Yes, I see similarities."

"But if Tom Lefroy was the model for Mr. Darcy—"

"I'm only speculating, of course." Martin nodded. "I'm

simply saying that elements from her own life might have inspired her."

I found the idea intriguing and more than a little scary. "And that's why her sister might have destroyed the first version? Because it was too close to what really happened?"

"Perhaps. Though I suppose we'll never know."

"Did Austen have other suitors?" I asked. "Why didn't she ever marry?"

"No one knows. There were vague references to other gentlemen, and her sister once said that Jane had indeed been in love, but in the end, it didn't work out."

"Oh."

Martin glanced at his watch. "Well, I'd better be going. I'm meeting an old friend for tea."

I looked up and blushed. "I'm sorry. I didn't mean to waylay you."

He waved a hand in dismissal. "Not at all. As you may have guessed, I'm a bit enamored of Jane Austen."

"It's always good to have a hobby."

For some reason that made him laugh. "You're right, of course." He paused, and the smile slid from his face to be replaced by a very sober expression. "Claire, I don't mean to intrude or be mysterious, but I feel like I should warn you to be wary. People you meet here aren't always what they seem. I find it's always best to be cautious."

He had no idea just how true that statement was, especially

when applied to me. "Martin? Is there something I should know about?" Was he giving me a specific warning or just feeling a bit paternal toward me?

He grimaced. "I'm sorry. Old habits die hard, I guess. As a father, I still worry about young women out in the world by themselves. Sorry if that seems old-fashioned."

"I appreciate your concern." Even if it did make me feel racked with guilt. After all, this was one of the people I'd led to believe that I was a doctor.

"I'll see you tonight for dinner in the Hall?" he asked.

"Sure." I smiled back.

He gave me a wave and slipped away between the stacks. I stayed where I was on the bench, thankful for a peaceful moment to consider everything I'd just learned.

Of course there was no way Harriet's papers could really be the missing manuscript, but what I'd learned from Martin troubled me. To know that such a version had existed...

And might still exist.

I didn't want to, but I had to admit to myself that there was a possibility that Harriet's manuscript might be authentic.

The heat. It had to be the heat, and it was frying my brain. I returned the book to the shelf and took a deep breath. Then I squared my shoulders and marched out of the store.

I was not going to let the ramblings of one confused woman ruin my Oxford experience. I had to let it go and not think about it anymore. Lost manuscripts, mysterious women, crumbling cottages—those were the stuff of fairy tales, not real life. I had learned long ago just how real, and painful, life could be. Now was not the time to forget. I would enjoy my time in Oxford, present Missy's paper as best I could, and try to quit lying to everyone I met.

Plain, straightforward goals were always best. Surely I could manage to achieve them over the course of the next week.

discovered on Monday morning that
the seminar room, like every other
part of the college, doubled as a sauna.
Some thoughtful soul had opened
the windows, but since not so much as a single breeze wafted
through them, the effort had been wasted. Dilapidated chairs
circled the threadbare rug. Empty bookshelves lined the walls.
For a tony Oxford college, the decor left something to be
desired. Then again it was a room primarily used by eighteen-
to-twenty-year-olds. Perhaps there was some wisdom in the
decorating scheme.

"Good morning." A woman with cropped gray hair and
bright hazel eyes rose from one of the straight-backed chairs.
"I'm Eleanor Gibbons. Welcome to the seminar."

"Thank you. I'm Claire Prescott." I looked around at the
empty spaces in the circle. "Am I that early?"

Eleanor glanced at her watch. "Not really. Let's just say that the atmosphere in the summer is a bit more relaxed than the traditional classroom."

"Oh." Great. I slid into the nearest chair and busied myself pulling a pen and notebook out of my tote bag. I'd been counting on a strong dose of traditional classroom structure to help me bluff my way through the week.

"So you're standing in for your sister, then?" Eleanor Gibbons said.

I nodded. "I'll try to keep up with the rest of the group."

She laughed. "You're already leading the pack," she said as she glanced at her watch again, "since you're the only one here on time."

"I skipped breakfast in the dining hall. I'm sure they'll be along any moment."

I'd barely slept the night before, a combination of jet lag and the agitation brought on by the incident with Harriet as well as my conversation with Martin. Not to mention James Beaufort. Consequently I'd slipped out Tom Gate shortly after seven o'clock that morning and found my way up the street to the closest Starbucks. It had been closed, of course. Apparently, Brits were much later risers than Americans. I couldn't think of a Starbucks in Kansas City that wouldn't be packed at that hour of the morning.

It had only taken ten minutes of standing with my nose pressed to the glass door for the sole barista on duty to take pity on me and let me in. Another ten minutes and one venti mocha later, I had found myself on the streets of Oxford, strolling aimlessly in solitary splendor. It wasn't a bad way to explore the city, as it turned out.

"Would you like to be the first presenter this morning?" Eleanor asked me.

I shook my head. "I'd rather not, if you don't mind."

She smiled and shook her head just enough to signal her bemusement. "I think you might be surprised—"

But then a shadow loomed in the doorway. James Beaufort.

I swallowed the groan that rose in my throat.

"Welcome," Eleanor said. He moved into the room as they made their introductions. He hadn't seen me yet, huddled in the corner.

"Thank you. I'm looking forward to the week." He was even more beautiful in profile than he was straight-on. I willed myself not to stare. Eleanor looked toward me. "This is Claire Prescott. She'll be glad of your company. It's a bad job being stranded with the tutor."

I wanted to sink through the chair bottom and then through the floor, but the laws of physics were not in my favor. I might as well have tattooed "Dateless and Desperate" on my forehead.

"We're already acquainted," James said as he seated himself two chairs away from me. A friendly if noncommittal distance. I hid my involuntary wince. He was definitely not interested in me.

I pasted a smile on my face. "Yes, we met yesterday."

Thankfully, voices sounded from the hallway, and in another moment, people flooded into the room. Eleanor moved forward to greet them. First were Rosie and Louise, two New Zealanders in their fifties with short hair and bright smiles, the first one plump and the other one quite spare. I'd met them at the welcome reception the previous evening after I returned from Blackwell's, and they'd quickly put me at ease. Next came Olga, a willowy Russian who had clearly taken a wrong turn on the way to the Miss Universe pageant. I was instantly aware of how my hair frizzed in the heat.

In addition to the three ladies, Eleanor welcomed two more men. Frank, a middle-aged cardiologist, and, of course, Martin.

"Shall we get started, then?" Eleanor said when everyone was seated. "I thought we would begin with the presentations straightaway. I know you will want plenty of time to discuss them."

The New Zealand ladies giggled, Martin rubbed his hands together as if anticipating a feast, and James Beaufort's spine stiffened even more, if such a thing were physically possible.

"I asked Claire if she would start us off," Eleanor continued, "but she's feeling a bit shy, so…"

Heat flooded my cheeks. I might as well have been twelve and walking into middle school for the first time, wearing the absolutely wrong outfit.

"If you need me to go first, I can." Years of unthinking

self-sacrifice gave voice to my words before I was even aware of forming them.

"We'll start," Rosie and Louise said in unison with matching gleams of eagerness in their eyes. Louise shivered with happiness. "We've been working on this for ages."

I made the mistake of looking up at that exact moment, and James's gaze caught mine. The expression there wasn't hard to read—amusement, irony, a dash of contempt. And to my horror, I returned the look and felt the zing of physical connection flash between us. He frowned at the unexpected spark and quickly looked away. I went back to blushing, which I apparently had down to an art form.

"We've chosen to make a presentation on the various incarnations of Mr. Darcy in film and television as well as in the book," Rosie said.

She shot Eleanor Gibbons an apprehensive look, and a knot formed in my stomach. My sister's obsession with Mr. Darcy was clearly shared by many women.

"I'm sure it will be fine," Eleanor said, and the anxiety disappeared from Rosie's face.

"Right. Well, then, we'll just begin."

She nodded to Louise, who reached into the bag next to her chair and pulled out a laptop. "We don't have a projector," Louise said, "but if you would all just gather round—"

"Gather round?" James said, sotto voce. His eyebrows climbed northward.

Rosie heard him but missed the sarcasm in his tone. "Rather than read a paper, we've made a video."

"A video?" Now Eleanor's eyebrows arched as well.

"It's not terribly long," Rosie reassured her, missing the point entirely. "Less than ten minutes."

Eleanor nodded with some reluctance. "Very well. Let's see if we can arrange ourselves."

We managed to clump the chairs together so that everyone could have a view of the screen. Somehow I wound up next to James, his upper arm pressed against mine as we squished together.

"We hope you enjoy it," Louise said gravely. She pressed the relevant keys and then scooted to stand behind the group.

Images flashed across the screen, accompanied by some gentle strains of instrumental music, and I recognized the pictures instantly. Mr. Darcy in all his depictions, from nineteenth-century pen-and-ink illustrations to Sir Laurence Olivier in the black-and-white film version. Then the modern-day incarnations—Colin Firth and Matthew Macfadyen, as well as other lesser-known ones. A woman's voice—I couldn't tell whether it was Rosie or Louise—provided the narration, and I desperately wished Missy were here instead of me.

"Mr. Darcy has undergone a variety of transformations in his existence," she began.

I wanted to flee the seminar room, but I had to stay and take notes for Missy. I swallowed the words I would have liked to say to my sister at that moment and focused instead on the pictures on the screen.

Physically, all the various incarnations of Mr. Darcy were different. Some tall, some shorter. Hair in various shades—although mostly brown. Noses of every shape. Soulful eyes, clear eyes, blue eyes, brown. Some chins pointed and others round. And yet all the pictures managed to capture some innate quality of Darcy-ness.

I thought then of the pages I'd read at Harriet's the day before. They hadn't included any mention of Mr. Darcy. What might Austen's original version of the character have been in that first effort? I'd always known he was a figure who transcended the novel that gave birth to him, but why? Because I certainly didn't get it. What was it about Mr. Darcy that made women swoon and sigh two centuries later? He wasn't the only compelling hero in the literary canon. Yet somehow he had captured the feminine imagination.

"So you see," Rosie's or Louise's voice concluded, "Mr. Darcy's place as an iconic hero will never be usurped."

Usurped? I made the mistake of glancing at James, and when our eyes met, that same palpable connection jumped to life between us again.

"I wasn't paying attention," I whispered to him as Louise put away the laptop. The others began to stand up and move their chairs into the original circle. "What did I miss?"

James snorted. "A lot of beefcake."

I barked with laughter and then turned away to hide my smile. Martin was looking at me with that twinkle in his eye, as if he knew I'd been woolgathering. I refrained from looking at Eleanor to see if she'd noticed my inattention as well.

The discussion that followed was genial but not very enlightening, and Eleanor's frustration was clear. I felt immensely relieved, though, and grateful for the standard that Rosie and Louise had set. Feeling far less intimidated, I even managed to contribute a thought or two of my own to the conversation. Still, I was relieved when Eleanor glanced at her watch and gave a signal for the midmorning break. Half a morning down, and only four and a half more to go. Perhaps there was hope for me yet.

❧❧❧❧❧

At the end of the morning, I had intended to hurry from the seminar room as soon as Eleanor dismissed us, but good manners required me to compliment Rosie and Louise on their presentation. Their informality had lifted a great weight from my shoulders, even if their subject matter wasn't my cup of tea.

By the time I escaped the heat of the seminar room for the even hotter atmosphere of the quad, my classmates had scattered. Near the door to the Junior Commons, I saw James and Eleanor in conversation. At first I thought it was a friendly chat, but they both looked very intense, and Eleanor's spine was extremely rigid. Most likely James was simply being his arrogant self. I turned to make my way to the Hall for lunch but hadn't taken two steps before I was stopped by Eleanor Gibbons calling my name.

She had left James standing alone on the walkway and was hurrying toward me. "Claire? Might I have a word?" Her hands fluttered, one of them clutching what appeared to be a letter.

"Yes?" Had I done something wrong? Made some faux pas in class that I wasn't aware of?

She stopped a few feet in front of me. Her mouth opened and closed twice before she finally spoke again.

"It's...um...well, it's rather a delicate matter, really."

I couldn't imagine what sort of matter, delicate or otherwise, might involve me, much less throw Eleanor for such a loop.

"Is everything okay?" The question sprang easily enough to my lips. Over the years I'd asked it multiple times a day—of Missy, of my co-workers, of pretty much anyone in my general vicinity.

Eleanor lifted the letter. Then, as if thinking the better of it, she crumpled the piece of paper in her hand. "Yes, yes. Everything's fine. It's just—" She drew a deep breath. "I understand you've made the acquaintance of one of our local eccentrics."

"Eccentrics?"

"Mrs. Dalrymple. I've just found this note from her in my mailbox."

"But she couldn't have had time to—"

"It wasn't posted. She put it in my faculty mailbox herself. So it's true, then? You've met her." Her eyes flashed with some unknown light—curiosity, fear, resignation.

I nodded, wondering what I'd gotten myself into. Some sort of local Jane Austen feud? Was Harriet in the habit of accosting Christ Church visitors on a regular basis?

"You shouldn't pay any attention to her ramblings," Eleanor was saying. "I'm afraid she has the beginnings of dementia."

"Oh." At her assertion, the air went out of me, as if I were a balloon and her words the pin. I'd known Harriet's manuscript couldn't be real, but I'd been intrigued...had been forced to wonder. But of course it was as fictional as...well...as fictional as one of Austen's novels. "Does she do this a lot? Take up with strangers?"

Eleanor shook her head. "Actually, no. And she's harmless enough, the old dear. Just a bit confused. She frightens some people. I'm sorry if she said anything to upset you."

"Upset me?" Eleanor's tone, placating but a little too ingratiating, made me wary. "Why would she upset me?"

Eleanor frowned. "Her delusions frighten some people."

"I wasn't frightened. She was nice enough to give me tea."

Eleanor didn't look comforted. "I'm sure she also gave you an earful about Jane Austen."

"Yes, but as you said, she's harmless enough."

Eleanor's dark eyes narrowed. Suddenly I found myself far more wary of her than of Harriet Dalrymple.

"It's best you give her a wide berth," Eleanor said. "She's written me babbling her nonsense again, but now she means to include you in it."

That was the moment when I knew that Eleanor Gibbons had something to hide. A secret that concerned Harriet Dalrymple. And me too, apparently.

"How do you know so much about her?" I had to ask. "Is she really such a nuisance?"

Eleanor's face softened then, and she looked as placid as she had when I'd entered the seminar room that morning.

"A nuisance?" She gave a dry chuckle. "No, Claire, she's not a nuisance. Far worse than that. Harriet Dalrymple is my mother."

ou do understand, don't you, why it's best to avoid her for the rest of your stay?" Eleanor gave me a stern look. "She's far more forgetful when she's agitated." She waved the letter in her hand. "Meeting you seems to have set her off again."

Remorse flooded through me. "I'm so sorry. I had no idea." However strangely Eleanor might be acting, I would never do anything to harm Harriet.

Eleanor nodded. "Of course you didn't. But now you know and can act accordingly."

She took a step along the pavement, and I followed her automatically. "Is it"—I wasn't even sure what to ask—"is it a permanent condition?" It sounded odd, but I meant well.

Eleanor hesitated. "She'll continue to have gradual memory loss. At some point, we'll have to make a change in her living situation. Find a place where she can be given the proper care."

I thought of Harriet's cottage in all its chaotic charm. "That will be difficult for her."

"Yes, it will." We had reached the gate beneath Tom Tower. "Thank you again for understanding. I know you'll abide by my wishes."

"But—" I would have liked to visit Harriet once more, at least to say good-bye.

Eleanor glanced at her watch. "Sorry, but I've got to rush. I'll see you in the morning."

Before I could ask any more questions or make a more formal plea to pay Harriet a farewell visit, Eleanor was gone.

I stood there for a moment, bewildered and unsure, and then I looked around the quad. It was surprisingly empty, except for James now standing nearby, hands in his pocket. He must have passed by me when Eleanor and I were talking at the gate. I flushed, since he had to have overheard our conversation.

"I'll see you at lunch," I said as I slid by him, embarrassed and intent on making a beeline for my room to freshen up and collect my thoughts.

"Claire, wait."

Surprise froze me in my tracks. I turned slowly back to him. "Yes?"

He paused and then colored—or at least I think he did. I found it difficult to tell given the heat.

"I wanted to ask you—" He obviously wasn't a man

accustomed to awkwardness, and I almost felt sorry for him. From the resigned look on his face, I thought he must need a favor. And he certainly didn't appear to be a man who liked to ask for help.

"Yes?"

"I'd like to take you to dinner tonight."

I resisted the urge to look over my shoulder and make sure he wasn't talking to someone standing just behind me.

"Dinner?" Not a very clever reply, but it was all I could manage at the time. Surprise—and abject fear—clogged my throat.

"The dining hall leaves a lot to be desired," he said, as if that were sufficient explanation for his unexpected offer. But I had actually enjoyed my meal the night before. Then again, I'd been rather distracted by my encounter with Harriet Dalrymple.

"Aren't we supposed to eat all our meals there?" I wondered if we were allowed "off campus."

"We're all adults," James said with a frown. "I don't think they take attendance or expel you. Besides"—he paused to grimace—"I've got to get out of here before I start using words like *prodigiously* in normal conversation."

I laughed.

"So will you go to dinner with me? I can have a taxi waiting at seven outside Tom Tower."

Well, I had come to Oxford for a little adventure, hadn't I?

"Seven o'clock," I repeated and he nodded, but the firm set of his mouth showed he'd never doubted my agreement.

"I'll see you then."

"Okay."

He was gone before I'd barely formed the word, striding off across the quad with a great sense of purpose. One minute he was, well, very Darcy-like, to tell the truth. Proud and haughty to the core. And the next moment he was reaching out and trying to establish a connection between us. No wonder Elizabeth Bennet had been so confused.

No wonder I was, too.

❧❧❧❧❧

The Cherwell Boathouse could have been any riverside pub, a gabled building of unremarkable brick and plaster that had stood the test of time. The cab pulled to a stop outside the entrance. James slid out and then turned and offered his hand to me. I placed my fingers in his palm and wondered if anyone had ever offered to help me out of a car before. I couldn't imagine Neil doing anything like it. And while I was as forward-thinking as any self-respecting American woman, the chivalrous gesture stirred something within me. I'd spent so much of my life taking care of other people that I never expected anyone to take care of me, even in such a small way.

Once I was on my feet on the pavement, James didn't release my hand but tucked it under his arm in an old-fashioned gesture and guided me toward the door. A hostess seated us outdoors on a broad terrace overlooking the river. Enormous trees arched overhead, shading us from the last of the day's heat. I still hadn't become accustomed to how late it stayed light.

James ordered a bottle of wine and a starter for both of us. I did bristle a little at his preemptive choice, but there was also an appeal to having the decision taken out of my hands. Still, I wasn't completely certain we were on a date, and so I planned to pay my own way. And my way would probably have been to choose a less expensive menu item, not to mention a budget bottle of wine.

"It's beautiful here," I said, looking around at the tranquil river and the willows that hung over it in a graceful bow. If I hadn't known better, I would never have guessed we were still in the city. "How did you find it?"

"The porter suggested it." The smile lines at the corners of his mouth showed me he was glad I'd approved his choice.

I smiled too, pleased that he'd gone to the trouble to get a recommendation and a reservation. Maybe we were on a date after all.

"You asked the right person, then." I gave a small, nervous laugh and then busied myself unwrapping my silverware and settling the napkin in my lap.

The waiter arrived with the wine, and James tasted and approved it. Our starter appeared a few moments later—seared king scallop with cauliflower puree, pea jelly, and lemongrass butter. A far cry from take-out barbecue with Neil while watching a Royals game. I took one bite and thought I'd achieved heavenly bliss. If the starter was this good, I could only imagine what the rest of the meal would be like.

We ate in silence for several minutes, lulled by the fading sunshine and the soft breeze in the trees. The tables on the terrace filled quickly, and soon we were surrounded by the soft hum of other people's conversation, punctuated by bursts of laughter. The clink of silverware and glassware accompanied the midsummer evensong.

"So, Claire, have you ever wanted to do anything besides practice medicine?" James lounged in his chair, one well-manicured hand resting on the pristine white tablecloth.

I felt a flush rise to my cheeks and tried to will it away. "Um, well, I suppose so. Doesn't everyone fantasize about their life being different?"

He leaned forward. "And what do you fantasize about?" He reached across the tablecloth and captured my hand in his. I was glad he'd taken hold of me. Otherwise I might have slid right out of my chair and onto the concrete terrace. I really was easy pickings.

"What about you?" Since I couldn't exactly answer honestly, I decided to turn the question on him. "Do you wish your life had turned out differently?"

He paused. "As you say, doesn't everyone?"

A shadow crossed his face, and for the first time, it occurred to me that he might have secrets of his own. Perhaps that was part of the appeal of a summer seminar like this, so far from home and reality. People could reinvent themselves, be whoever they wanted others to see instead of who they truly were. Such deep and potentially dangerous thoughts could only lead to unwanted self-examination, so I took a hearty drink of my wine and tried to focus on the breathtakingly handsome man across from me.

"I can't imagine that anything about your life is less than perfect." I tried to smile flirtatiously but probably only looked as if I was in a moderate amount of pain.

"I'm flattered that you've imagined anything about me." He squeezed my hand. "I like the sound of that."

To a more worldly woman, a woman with more experience with men, the words might have sounded as slick and self-serving as they were. But to me, at that point in time, they were like balm on a wound I'd never realized I had. I'd never been one to seek out flattery, which was what made me so susceptible. I'd known that most women were better looking than I was, were more successful, had more education.

Maybe that's why I'd ended up with Neil. He was nothing extraordinary. His very ordinariness had been his main attraction.

And then I felt another blush rise to my cheeks, but this time the heat was from shame, not attraction. Neil deserved better. Certainly he wasn't the most attentive of boyfriends, but he was a decent guy, patient and good-natured.

"Have you always worked in publishing?" I said to cover my own discomfort. "It sounds very cerebral."

He waved his free hand in dismissal. "Pretty routine. Dreary, really. But it pays the bills."

So much for that line of conversation. I took another sip of water and tried again. "What's your topic for your presentation?"

He shrugged. "I'm not sure."

"You haven't written your paper yet?" My eyes must have been bulging out in a most unattractive manner.

"After today's fan-girl video, I'm not too worried."

I had to laugh, but I also felt a little bit ashamed. Rosie and Louise were such dears, and their work had come from a deep devotion to Austen's hero.

"You didn't enjoy the Mr. Darcy retrospective?" I asked in a teasing tone.

"That's an awful lot for an average guy to live up to," he said before reaching to refill our wine glasses. "All that nobility. Not to mention wealth."

"I'm not exactly Darcy's biggest fan, but I've watched my sister swoon, and I don't think money's the appeal." Although with my recent change in circumstances, I could now understand Jane Austen's concerns about personal finance more personally.

"You don't think it's the money?" He half smiled and half grimaced. "You can't separate Darcy from his wealth. He could never have forced Wickham to marry Lydia without his power and influence, or his cash."

I opened my mouth to refute his assertion, but then I realized that he was right. "Um…"

"There's no arguing with that. I don't hold it against you, though."

"Against me?"

He nodded. "Not you personally. Women in general. Some things may have changed in the last two centuries, but I don't think a woman's wanting a man to look after her has gone completely out of style."

"I would never expect—"

He stopped me by the simple expedience of placing his thumb against my lips. The gesture was both frustrating and disturbingly sensual. "I know you wouldn't. That's one of the reasons I asked you out."

"Oh." I had no idea what to say after that. Fortunately, our entrées arrived at just that moment, and I could busy myself with the business of eating while I tried to sort through my churning thoughts and feelings.

We were on a date. He liked that I was independent. And I quivered like a big bowl of Jell-O whenever he touched me. Beyond that, I wasn't sure I was very coherent.

"So who do you think will volunteer to present tomorrow?" I said, trying to steer the conversation back to a neutral subject.

James chewed for a moment and then swallowed. "Martin, I hope. He should have something more than swooning admiration of Mr. Darcy to contribute to the conversation."

"I ran into him in the bookstore yesterday. He's quite the Austen devotee."

James paused in the act of cutting his food and gave me a strange look. "You don't know?" He laughed, a little too much at my expense, but he smiled too, and my heart fluttered. "Martin came to Oxford to be a visiting professor in the fall. He's one of the world's leading Austen scholars. I don't know why he's part of our seminar, though. He must be bored to tears among such a collection of amateurs."

"A professor?" But he hadn't looked bored, I thought with some surprise. In fact, of all the people in the room, he'd seemed the most delighted with Rosie and Louise's fan video. A new knot formed in my stomach, taking up residence with all the others that had formed there since my arrival at Christ Church. At the rate they were moving in, they'd need to form a homeowner's association before long.

"He's an expert? On Jane Austen?" And then it occurred to me that Martin was the very man I needed. He would know if Harriet Dalrymple's manuscript was the real thing.

The thought came out of nowhere just as I swallowed a bite of lemon sole. I gasped and then started coughing, pressing my napkin against my mouth to keep from spraying James with fish.

"Are you okay?" He was out of his chair and next to mine in an instant. "Claire? What can I do?"

His furrowed brow and the concern in his eyes made it even more difficult to breathe, but I managed. I waved my hand toward his chair and kept the napkin firmly against my lips.

"I'm okay," I gasped between coughing jags.

He stepped cautiously around the table and took his seat again, but he was eyeing me as if I were a grenade that might detonate at any moment.

"Really. I'm fine now." My voice was weak but otherwise normal. I took a sip of water. "I'm sorry. I didn't mean to cause a scene."

He looked around. "No one's watching." He reached across the table, and his fingers brushed mine where I was clenching the stem of the water goblet. His touch flustered me, and I could barely disguise the fact. I hoped he would attribute my flushed face to the choking incident.

"I can usually eat a meal without requiring medical attention."

"But you have a doctor on call everywhere you go," he said with a smile.

"What?"

"You have a doctor wherever you go." He nodded toward me. And then I caught on. Which almost sent me into another coughing fit.

"Um…yeah," I said in a strangled voice. "I guess so." My pulse leaped in my throat, and I could only pray that no one would fall to the ground in need of medical attention before we could finish our dinner and leave.

❧❧❧❧❧

My misery was my own fault, of course. I was on eggshells in James's presence, since I had to be on guard not to say anything that might expose me for the liar I was. By the time we arrived back at Christ Church, I just wanted to escape to my room. The pretense of being a completely different person was far more exhausting than I could have ever imagined.

We crossed beneath Tom Gate and came out into the bare quad.

"Well, good night," I said. I resisted the urge to stick out my right hand for him to shake. "Thank you for dinner. It was wonderful." My whole body felt as stiff and fragile as the words I was saying.

James looked at me with a curious expression. "Can I walk you to your room?"

"Oh no. It's four flights up for nothing." And then I blushed like a teenager. Because of course I'd just told him that any potential good-night kiss at my door was nothing. "I mean—"

"Are you normally this nervous, or is it just around me?" He quirked one eyebrow and smiled.

I melted. "I'm sorry. It's just that I haven't done this in a long time."

"Done what? Stood outdoors talking to a man?" His tone was teasing but gentle. He seemed to have so many sides to him—taciturn one moment, charming the next. But which one was the real James Beaufort?

I shook my head. "Dated. I haven't dated in quite a while." Which was one of the truest things I'd said all evening. Neil and I either went to one of his softball games or watched some sporting event on television. We hadn't been out to dinner in months, and I usually ended up cooking something at my apartment and taking it with me to his house.

"Men in Kansas City are idiots." He lifted a hand and cupped my cheek. "We've got all week, Claire. Don't worry about it."

Gratitude, relief, and regret swamped me. Gratitude for his understanding. Relief that he didn't think I was a complete weirdo. And regret that I'd spurned his good-night kiss.

"I'll see you in the morning?" I said, half statement and half question.

He nodded. "All Jane Austen, all the time."

I giggled, a sound I hadn't made in a very long time. And before I could do or say anything else to embarrass myself, I stepped away from him. "Good night."

"Good night, Claire." He was so incredibly handsome, standing there in the fading light. Not to mention my heart ache.

An unexpected sob rose in my throat, but I turned and hurried across the quad before it could burst free.

Whatever I was feeling at that moment, I again had only myself to blame. The thought provided no comfort at all as I raced back to my room and a long night with a guilty conscience.

he next afternoon found me following the riverside path once more toward Harriet Dalrymple's cottage. I had debated going there for most of the morning during Olga's presentation on Jane Austen's view of the British navy and then during the cardiologist's graphically detailed account of Jane Austen's struggle with Addison's disease. Both had been fairly interesting, but the appearance of Jane Austen in the flesh wouldn't have been enough to distract me from my dilemma.

Oddly enough, the dark looks Eleanor Gibbons kept shooting my way finally made the decision for me. If the problem was merely Harriet's dementia, I didn't think Eleanor would seem so upset. No, the situation was far more complicated than simply a worried daughter and an ailing mother.

I approached Harriet's cottage with trepidation. Perhaps she would turn me away after my abrupt and ungracious departure on Sunday. Still, I had to try. I lifted a hand to knock on the blue door, but it opened before I could make contact with the brightly painted wood.

"Claire!" Harriet's round face glowed, and she smiled at me as if greeting a long-lost friend. "You've returned." Her eyes actually twinkled. "I thought you might, once you'd had time to think it over."

"I'm sorry if I was rude the other day," I said as she waved me over the threshold and into the cottage. "It was all just rather—"

"Overwhelming. I know. But now you've seen sense and we can proceed."

"Proceed?" Wariness sent a quick chill down my spine.

"With more of the manuscript. I assume that's why you're here. You know what they say about curiosity, my dear."

"Um, that it's a leading cause of death among felines?"

Harriet laughed, a scratchy but melodious sound, like a vinyl record that had seen better days but still retained its tune. "Well done, my dear. Well done. Now, come through to the sitting room and let me see if I can find another chunk of that manuscript for you."

That manuscript? Were there others? What if Harriet's cottage held more than one undiscovered treasure? My eyes darted over objects as we made our way down the short hallway and into the sitting room. Only Harriet knew what all of the cabinets, baskets, and boxes contained, and even she might not still remember what was there.

"Sit here again." She patted the sofa with the broken springs. "Let me find those pages, and then I'll make some tea. I set them aside for when you came back…"

I perched with care on the sagging cushion nearest me. "Harriet, would you mind answering a question?"

She was riffling through the desk at the end of the room. She looked back at me over her shoulder. "Not at all, dear. What would you like to know?"

"You said you were left the manuscript. If it's not too nosy, I was wondering who your benefactor was."

Her hands paused in the act of searching. She straightened and turned toward me.

"Yes, yes. I suppose this is as good a time to tell you as any. Oh, there it is!" She moved across the room with amazing alacrity for a woman her age. She picked up a pile of yellowed pages from a bookshelf crammed with volumes of every shape, size, and description. "That's the next bit I wanted you to read."

She crossed to the sofa and handed me the papers. Then she sat down next to me. "I wasn't sure whether to tell you before. You seemed so agitated."

Agitated was an understatement, but I didn't reply. Instead, I waited for her to speak her piece.

"Very few people have ever seen these," she began. She

tapped the manuscript in my lap. "It's an honor, you see, but also a responsibility. A very great responsibility." She sounded like one of my young nieces when they shared a secret with me, solemn and excited all at the same time.

"I appreciate you including me," I said, although *appreciate* might not have been quite the right word.

"Mrs. Parrot won't like that I've shown you this," she said in a softer tone, as if she were afraid someone might be listening to us. I glanced around the gentrified chaos of Harriet's sitting room. For all I knew, someone might be listening. In Harriet's cottage, anything seemed possible.

"Mrs. Parrot?"

"Yes. She's in charge, you know."

"No. I didn't know that." My shoulders sagged. Eleanor had been telling the truth after all. Harriet clearly wasn't quite in touch with reality.

Harriet laid a gnarled hand on my forearm. "Yes, well, I had promised her not to act without her sanction. It was one of her conditions."

"Conditions?"

"For allowing me into the group."

I wanted to tell her right then that I knew about her dementia. That Eleanor had spilled the beans. That this Mrs. Parrot was probably a figment of her imagination—or rather, her illness. But Harriet was so sweet and harmless, really. Why not humor her some more?

"So this Mrs. Parrot, she calls the shots?"

Harriet nodded. "They've kept her secrets for many years, you see. Almost two centuries."

I paused, confused. "They? Kept secrets? Whose secrets?"

"Why, Jane Austen's, of course."

I suppressed the laugh that threatened to escape. "What are you? Part of some secret society?"

"Yes, exactly." She beamed at me. "We're called the Formidables."

I had been joking, but Harriet clearly wasn't. "The What-ables?"

"The Formidables. It's the name Jane Austen and her sister, Cassandra, gave themselves in their later years. All the nieces and nephews called them by that name."

From what I had heard of Austen's character, I could imagine that she had been a very formidable maiden aunt indeed. "And it's a secret group?" Perhaps it was best to humor her and then make my escape as quickly as I could.

Harriet smiled. "Very secret. And very exclusive."

Her disclosure took the wind out of my sails. Harriet's mind was as charming and disordered as her cottage. Secret society indeed.

"Why would Jane Austen need protection?" I couldn't help but ask. "What secrets could she possibly have had?"

Harriet pursed her lips just a touch. "You might be surprised, if you knew." She looked as if she wanted to say more on the subject, but instead she tapped the manuscript pages in my lap. "The Formidables require absolute discretion." She looked up and I met her gaze. It was clear as crystal, with no sign of mental deterioration.

"Then why are you sharing your secret with me?"

Harriet smiled. "I knew I could rely on your keeping this matter confidential."

"How could you know that?" Guilt poured through me.

Harriet sniffed. "By looking at you, of course. I am a superior judge of character."

I couldn't bring myself to disillusion her.

Harriet's smile wavered. "I need your help, you see."

"My help?"

She placed the crumbling pages in my hands. "We'll talk more about that later. For now, go ahead and read, my dear. I'll see to the tea."

She rose from the sofa and disappeared from the sitting room, leaving me alone with the stack of yellowed pages and my own confusion. I looked down and started to read.

First Impressions
Chapter Three

Chapter Three? I looked up, wanting to ask Harriet where the missing second chapter might be, but she was already in the kitchen. I could hear her running water and rattling dishes.

Lady Catherine proved to be a tireless employer who never failed to find fault with Elizabeth's efforts. Miss de Bourgh was slightly less trying and only showed her displeasure by coughing behind her handkerchief when overset.

Lady Catherine? Miss de Bourgh? Employers?

No, that was completely wrong. The Lady Catherine in *Pride and Prejudice* was Darcy's aunt. But then I remembered that the chapter I'd read on Sunday mentioned Elizabeth seeking employment. Was that how Austen had first envisioned it, then? That Darcy and Elizabeth would meet at Lady Catherine's home, Rosings?

"We are to have visitors today," Lady Catherine announced at breakfast over toast and coffee. "My dear nephews cannot keep away." She cast a pointed glance at her daughter. "There is much at Rosings to tempt them, you see."

Anne de Bourgh raised her napkin and coughed. Elizabeth took a bite of her toast as a means of hiding the smile that threatened. She chewed and then sipped her coffee. "Your nephews, Lady Catherine?"

Her inquiry gratified her employer's vanity.

"Yes, such dear boys. They are quite attached to Rosings. And to me," she added for emphasis as she waved away the footman who would have removed her plate. "Mr. Darcy of Pemberley in Derbyshire. And Colonel Fitzwilliam, grandson of the Earl of _____, with a

comfortable independence. I expect that they will stay a month altogether. Perhaps two."

Yes, there was Darcy, all right. And Colonel Fitzwilliam too, although he was a very minor character in *Pride and Prejudice*. I had wondered, when I read the novel, why Austen hadn't done more with him.

Elizabeth couldn't imagine any inducement that would lure two young gentlemen into such a lengthy visit, but she knew better than to express her opinion.

"We must provide them with some little entertainments." Lady Catherine's eyes narrowed. "Dinner parties, to be sure. Perhaps a picnic, if the weather holds." She looked at her daughter. "I should like to give a ball, Anne, if you think your health sufficient to the demands." Lady Catherine's expression clearly conveyed her wishes on the matter to her daughter.

"Of course, Mama. Whatever you like."

Elizabeth would have liked nothing more than to intervene. Anne's health was too delicate, of course, for such exertions, but Elizabeth had learned in her weeks at Rosings that to contradict Lady Catherine only made her more obstinate.

"A ball, ma'am?" Elizabeth said. "I can think of nothing more enjoyable."

Lady Catherine's eyebrows tilted until they nearly met

her hairline. "Enjoyable? I assure you, Miss Bennet, my motive is not to provide my daughter's companion with a party of pleasure."

Elizabeth schooled her features into a servile expression. "Of course not, ma'am. I only meant—"

"What you meant is of no importance to me. Your presence will be necessary only when Anne has need of you. Otherwise, you shall remain in your room, well out of the way."

"Of course, ma'am."

Even though she had become accustomed to Lady Catherine's imperious manner, her contempt still did injury to Elizabeth's pride.

"I'm a little tired, Mama," Anne said. "I think I shall return to my room to rest."

"You are looking peaked." Lady Catherine frowned at Elizabeth as if she were the cause of her daughter's distress. "Perhaps you might try to make her comfortable, Miss Bennet, if it is not too much trouble."

"I shall put my whole heart into the task," Elizabeth said with as sweet a smile as her disposition could muster. "Anne? Take my arm. We will call for a footman to assist us, if one is needed."

Anne did as Elizabeth said and leaned heavily against her. "Thank you, dearest Lizzie."

"Lizzie?" Lady Catherine's shock rang in her voice. "Such familiarity—"

"I asked if I might call her that, Mama," Anne said as she sagged a bit more.

Lady Catherine harrumphed but returned her attention to her coffee.

"Come, Anne." Elizabeth helped her from the room and wondered which might be worse—an imperious mother or an ineffectual one. Intimacy with Lady Catherine de Bourgh was rapidly improving Mrs. Bennet in Elizabeth's estimation.

"Here is the tea, Claire."

Harriet's voice jerked me back into the present moment. I looked up at her in confusion. "Elizabeth is at Rosings as a paid companion? That's not what happened in the book." Dismay and frustration had settled on me like a veil as I read the pages.

Harriet set the tea tray on the table in front of the sofa. "Yes, the plot is very different, is it not?"

I looked helplessly at the manuscript in my lap. "It's not right. Elizabeth shouldn't be there."

"Right? I suppose not. But that is how matters stand. At least on these pages."

I peered at her. "Is it true? Is this the missing early manuscript? Is it the real *First Impressions?*"

Harriet shrugged and reached for the teapot, but I could see she was quite enjoying herself. "What do you think?" She handed me a cup of fragrant tea, and I gripped it carefully so I wouldn't spill any on the pages in my lap.

"I don't know," I said.

"Then you must keep reading," Harriet said. "Perhaps further acquaintance will help you decide."

I took a sip of the tea and did as she'd instructed, confused but also excited, and worried that I was allowing myself to be caught up in a sweet, dotty woman's fantasy.

CHAPTER TEN

First Impressions
Chapter Four

The park at Rosings proved ample to Elizabeth's need
for respite from her employer. As soon as Anne had fallen
into a sound sleep, Elizabeth slipped from the room and
made her way to her own chamber under the eaves near
the other servants' quarters. There, she donned her bonnet
and pelisse. Anne would no doubt sleep for several hours,
as was her custom. Elizabeth said a prayer of thanksgiving
for the fine weather and made her way out of the house.

She called a greeting to the head groomsman as
she passed the stables and then set out down the path
that wound its way through the park. The sunshine held
more promise of warmth than the actuality of it, but the
brilliance of the sky and the carpet of bluebells beneath
the trees heralded the arrival of spring.

She had climbed the rise behind the house and achieved the overlook when she heard a horse approaching from the opposite direction. She stepped to the side of the path. No doubt it was one of the grooms exercising his mount. Yet when beast and rider came into view, she recognized neither the man nor the animal.

The dark-haired stranger reined the horse to a stop a few yards away and looked at her down the length of his aristocratic nose. No doubt some would call his visage handsome, but Elizabeth saw only arrogance. She curled her fingers into soft fists at her side and hid her much worn and mended gloves in the folds of her skirts.

"Good day, sir." She had no apprehension of danger, for she was near enough to the house. Still, given her sheltered upbringing at Longbourn, she had little experience meeting strangers and so exercised caution.

"Good day." He bowed at her greeting but offered her no acknowledgement as his equal.

Silence fell while Elizabeth waited for him to elaborate or explain himself. Instead, he seemed inclined to sit mutely atop his horse. Whoever he was, she thought very little of his manners and breeding. Even in the restricted society of Meryton, men knew how to be chivalrous when meeting a lady.

She glanced down at her decidedly unfashionable pelisse and felt the weight of her rather plain bonnet, as if it were made of iron rather than straw and ribbon. She supposed he took her for a servant, which, in truth, she was. As such, she should no doubt nod, duck her head, and scurry past. But Lady Catherine's harangue at the breakfast table still nettled her, as did this gentleman's stiff-necked posture.

"You are bound for Rosings, sir?" She spoke the words before her better judgment could persuade her to hold her tongue.

His eyebrows rose in surprise at her familiarity. "I am, madam, though I am sure it is no concern of yours. You would be better served to concede the path."

He might have been a Spanish matador waving a crimson cape, so effectively did his words stoke her temper.

"I thought I already had, sir." She glanced down at her sturdy boots, now wet with morning dew where she stood in the grass. "But perhaps I expect too much. A gentleman would not leave a lady standing in the damp while he lectured her."

He stiffened, as if she'd dealt him a blow.

"Good day, sir." Elizabeth stepped onto the path in defiance of him.

His jaw tightened, and she suppressed a smile. But then the expression of triumph that threatened died an instant death. For she realized in that moment that the man before her must be one of Lady Catherine's nephews.

ell, Mr. Darcy, at least, was very much the same, I thought as I turned the page. His pride was as evident in this version of the book as in the later one. Perhaps, in the end, Austen hadn't changed that much from the early version.

> *"Headstrong, impetuous girl."* Lady Catherine's favorite imprecation against Elizabeth rang in her ears. Her employer was right, of course. No matter how Elizabeth tried to curb her behavior, she was too accustomed to speaking her own mind to prevent it happening.
>
> She hurried away from the gentleman at such a pace that her feet seemed barely to touch the ground. Had it been the Mr. Darcy of Pemberley she'd just insulted? She rather thought so, since he'd not appeared to be a military man. True, his bearing had been just short of regal, but he hadn't the demeanor of a soldier who had campaigned in the saddle.
>
> With a sigh, and a short prayer that her impertinence would not put paid to her tenure as Anne's companion, Elizabeth hurried along the path as quickly as her dew-slickened boots would allow.

"Her first encounter with Darcy doesn't go well," I said, looking up at Harriet. "That much hasn't changed. He insults her in the park instead of in public, at the Meryton assembly."

Harriet nodded. "True. That much is the same." She reached for the plate of cookies on the tea tray. "Biscuit?" she said as she offered me my choice of the stale-looking tidbits.

"No, I'm fine, thanks." I bent my head once more to avoid her insisting that I help myself. From the looks of them, the cookies were as old as one of my nieces.

The park that day was destined to be her comeuppance, Elizabeth decided, when not long after her encounter with Mr. Darcy she came upon yet another gentleman seated on a fallen log just off the path. He wore riding clothes, but she saw no evidence of a horse. Although he was not old by any means, his face was tanned by the sun. His weather-beaten complexion confirmed his identity.

"Good day, sir."

He rose at her approach and doffed his hat, the very antithesis of the man she'd met a few moments before. "Good day, madam." He grinned rather sheepishly, an attractive expression that emphasized the laugh lines at the corners of his eyes. "Please take no fright at my appearance. My horse got the better of me and left me stranded here. I had hoped for a rescue party, and here you are."

"Are you injured, Colonel Fitzwilliam?" Elizabeth asked with a smile, unable to conceal her knowledge.

He responded in kind with laughter of his own. "You must be Miss Elizabeth Bennet. My aunt mentioned you in her letters."

"I am quite certain she must have." Elizabeth clasped her gloved hands in front of her. "I am afraid that I am a great trial to Lady Catherine."

"Yes, well, my aunt could use a few more trials, I think." He paused. "But where are my manners? You will think me the veriest slowtop." He pushed himself to his feet, but once there, he wavered.

"Sir, you are injured." Elizabeth moved to his side. "Put your hand on my shoulder."

"One might think a cavalry officer would be capable of remaining in the saddle. I have been too long absent from my regiment."

"You have returned from the Continent, sir?" Elizabeth's respect for him grew. "Have you served there long?"

"Long enough, Miss Elizabeth." He glanced down at one scuffed boot, as weathered as his complexion. "I am afraid that my ankle will not support me as far as the house."

"It is a shame that it is only I, and not your cousin, who happened upon you."

"My cousin? So you've made Darcy's acquaintance, have you? He always did manage to best me in a race."

"I met him on the path only five minutes ago, but I

fear he will be at the house by now. I wonder you did not see him yourself."

Colonel Fitzwilliam gave her another sheepish grin. "I took off across the countryside rather than remain safely on the road. I thought to steal a march on Darcy, but my treachery has demanded payment."

"Treachery?" Elizabeth laughed. "I have no brothers, Colonel, but I suspect you suffer more from the affliction of rivalry usually associated with close siblings. Nothing as dire as treachery."

The colonel nodded. "Yes, perhaps that's the case." He looked around. "Well, Miss Elizabeth Bennet, I am afraid you must be my means of rescue. Would you be so kind as to make your way back to the house and send a stout groom with a fresh horse? And perhaps spread the word that my own mount is loose somewhere in the park?"

Elizabeth bit her lip. "I do not like to leave you here alone, sir."

His eyes sparkled. "And I do not wish it either, ma'am, but it cannot be helped."

Elizabeth flushed. She had not meant to flirt. She had learned long ago to leave such behavior to Kitty and Lydia. But the admiration in the colonel's eyes was balm to a soul that had begun to sink beneath the weight of Lady Catherine's disapprobation.

"I will walk as quickly as possible," she assured him and turned to go.

"Not too quickly," he called after her. *"For if you fall and injure yourself, we are both undone."*

Elizabeth chuckled and hurried back along the path from where she had come. Since she did not turn to look back at the colonel, she failed to see the admiration in his eyes and the warmth with which he regarded her retreating form.

"Colonel Fitzwilliam?" I looked up at Harriet in astonishment. "He's Darcy's rival for Elizabeth?"

Harriet nodded, an impish smile on her face. "In this version, yes."

"But he's barely mentioned at all in the real novel." My protest only widened Harriet's smile.

"The *real* novel? But aren't these pages *real?*"

"You know what I mean." Irritation pinched at my spine. "This isn't what really happened. Jane Austen obviously changed her mind about a lot of things when she rewrote it."

"Obviously."

Harriet's nodding agreement only spurred my irritation. "So this is just an early draft. It doesn't change the outcome, does it?" I assumed Harriet had long since read the manuscript.

"The outcome?" She paused.

I bit my lip in frustration. "Whatever happens, Darcy and Elizabeth have to end up together." I stopped then and remembered why I was seated on Harriet's lumpy sofa in the first place. I needed to placate her, not fuss at her.

Harriet eyed me with some interest. "Why should it bother you if Elizabeth fancies Colonel Fitzwilliam?"

"Because it's not the right ending. I mean, I know she and Mr. Darcy don't hit it off at first, but he improves upon acquaintance."

"What of Mr. Wickham, though?" Harriet asked. "Doesn't Elizabeth fall prey to his charms? He's Darcy's rival in the final version."

I shook my head. "But he's a scoundrel, and Colonel Fitzwilliam isn't. Elizabeth might have had her head turned a bit by Wickham, but..."

"Perhaps in this version, the choice is not so simple, between a gentleman and a rogue. Perhaps Elizabeth must decide between two worthy men."

"Two worthy men?" I echoed, a note of despair in my voice. Trying to figure out one man was difficult enough.

Harriet nodded. "That's rather a more complicated task, isn't it?"

I opened my mouth to speak and realized I had no idea what to say.

"Perhaps if you come back tomorrow," Harriet said, "I'll have found the next bit of manuscript."

"It's not all in one spot?" That explained why she only handed me one section at a time.

"It's here somewhere." She waved a hand at the chaos in the room. "It's not as if it will grow feet and wander off, is it?" she asked with a smile.

"But..." I wanted to tell her about Eleanor and confess that I was there against her daughter's wishes, but I hesitated. Instead, I picked up the pages and handed them back to Harriet.

"Thank you for letting me read this." I leaned down to pick up my purse from the floor beside my feet.

"Wait." Harriet's expression grew serious. "You can't leave yet. Not until you tell me what you think."

Oh dear. "I'm just here to visit," I said. "And I really ought to be going."

"But I need someone." Her hands tightened on the manuscript pages. "I need you to help me decide what to do with the manuscript."

"Why don't you just keep it here?"

I hoped that might placate her, but Harriet rose from the sofa and walked to the window. She unearthed a handkerchief in her pocket and clutched it in her hands. "I can't..." She broke off and then took a deep breath and seemed to collect herself. "I won't be able to take care of it for much longer, so Mrs. Parrot thinks it's best if I give it to her."

The grief and frustration etched in her face brought tears to my eyes, and I wished for a handkerchief of my own.

"Mrs. Parrot? The head of the Formidables? She's pressuring you to give it to her?"

"Yes, but Eleanor wants it too. She says it's her birthright."

"So Eleanor knows about *First Impressions*?" Goosebumps rose on my arms. The Formidables might be fictional, but Eleanor was very real indeed. If she thought this manuscript was the real thing...

Harriet nodded. "I only told her very recently. She was

furious. Said I had no right to keep it from her. She didn't under-stand, you see, about the Formidables. About keeping secrets."

"Oh." What could I say? "Are there others, then, who know about it?"

Harriet shook her head. "They suspect, but very few really know."

"But what if it isn't——" I stopped. I didn't want to agitate Harriet any further.

"If it isn't real?" She gave me a watery smile. "Sometimes I wish that it weren't. My life would certainly be more peaceful."

A knock sounded at the front door. Harriet pulled back the curtain and peered out the window.

"Oh dear." She dropped her handkerchief on the window-sill and then quickly drew the curtain.

"Harriet? Is something wrong?" I wondered who she'd seen that caused her so much distress.

"It's Mrs. Parrot. She's come back again to try and talk me out of the manuscript." Harriet looked wildly around the room. "Here, quickly." She grabbed the pages I'd been reading from the low table by the sofa and shoved them at me. "Hide these." Then she bustled off, grabbing another stack of pages from the top of her writing desk and still another from the bookshelves.

Mrs. Parrot knocked again at the door while I moved to fol-low Harriet around the room. She continued to stack the pages in my arms. I didn't know what else to do, so I slipped them as carefully as possible into my oversized purse.

"There's more, but I can't remember where I've put them." Harriet cast me a desperate look.

"Don't worry. I'll take good care of them," I said, my heart racing. She was really going to let me walk out of there with one of the world's greatest secrets in my bag. "But won't she suspect I've taken them?"

Harriet grimaced. "She might, but she won't know for sure. You can hide them in your room at the college. They'll be safe enough there."

I hoped so. *I hoped so?* That was the moment when I realized that Harriet had won me over. I believed her, and I was going to help her, no matter how much Eleanor berated me.

"You can slip out the back," Harriet said. She put a hand on my back and motioned toward the door to the sitting room. "Through the kitchen garden, then to the right on the path. It will take you back to the river."

"Okay." I stopped and turned to look at her. "Will you be all right? I can stay. You don't have to face her alone."

Harriet shook her head. "I'll be fine. Much better now that I know the manuscript is in good hands." She laughed. "I haven't had this much excitement in years. It's quite exhilarating, really."

I had to laugh too, although I was afraid that mine held a tinge of hysteria. "I'll be back tomorrow," I promised her.

"Of course you will." Harriet beamed at me.

Her complete faith in me was almost my undoing. "Thank you, Harriet. For trusting me."

She waved both hands, shooing me toward the back door. "Of course I trust you. Now go."

I did as she told me and slipped through the kitchen and out the door. The latch on the back garden gate proved a bit tricky, but finally my fumbling fingers succeeded in getting it open. I set off down the small path at a brisk trot, hoping that I'd done the right thing. On this side of the Atlantic, the right thing seemed a whole lot harder to figure out than it had been back home.

 clutched my purse close to me. It felt as if it were covered with a label that said "Secret Jane Austen Manuscript" in large neon letters. Blinking ones, in fact. The people I passed during my return walk along the river, though, didn't seem to notice. I reached the King's Walk and made a beeline for Christ Church. If I could only reach my room and stash the pages there. Then I could sit down and figure out what to do.

As it turned out, I couldn't even escape to my room. I was almost to the end of the graveled walk when I saw James sitting on the same large stump where I'd first met Harriet. He saw me too, and the taut lines of his face eased to something resembling pleasure. What was he doing there? I bit back the panic that rose in my throat and pasted a smile on my face.

"Hello," I said with what I hoped sounded like the right amount of casual surprise and not simply abject terror. "Are you enjoying your afternoon?"

He smiled. "I'm bored. I came looking for you. What are you up to?"

"I...um...well, I just..." How had he known where to find me?

He shot me a teasing look. "You sound like you're up to no good."

"Me?" I tried not to squeak. "No, I was just...visiting a friend."

"You have friends in Oxford?" Now he was the one who looked surprised.

"I just met her the other day."

"Her?" His face relaxed into lines of relief. At least I thought they were lines of relief. "Who is she?"

I fanned my face, grateful for the actual heat that disguised the elevated temperature of my emotions. "An older lady. I met her right here, actually. She was selling some greeting cards she'd made."

"How was your visit?" He watched me intently, searching for something in my face.

"Very nice." I resisted the urge my pull my bag closer to me. "Shall we?" I gestured up the path, away from Harriet's cottage.

He stood up and came toward me. "I wanted to check out the university's Botanic Garden. Would you like to come with me?"

The manuscript made my purse feel as if it weighed a ton. I would dearly have loved to stash the pages in my room, but James was standing in front of me, making my pulse race again, and I couldn't bring myself to turn down the opportunity to spend time with him.

"Okay."

He stepped onto the path, and we started walking. My heart rate hadn't slowed a bit.

"So tell me more about your friend," he said as we made our way back toward Christ Church and then alongside the meadow that separated it from the river. The cows stood somnolent amid the dry grass, inert in the heat.

"My friend? Oh, you mean Harriet." I couldn't look at him when I answered. "She's just a harmless old lady, I guess. She has the most amazing cottage, though. Full of knickknacks."

"Sounds like your average grandmother."

"If your average grandmother lived somewhere that looked like it was painted by Beatrix Potter." I smiled and tried not to look as guilty as I felt.

✿✿✿✿✿

The Botanic Garden was ripe with the fragrances of summer—honeysuckle and newly mown grass. I wanted to stop and smell the roses, quite literally, but James sped down the path as if he were power walking instead of playing tourist.

We were making our way through the famous walled garden, where large rectangles created by the footpaths housed different families of plants. Since it was a scientific garden, every bit of flora was clearly labeled. I'd read somewhere that there were more than eight thousand kinds of plants kept there, and I wondered who had the job of making all the labels. At my office, making the labels for all the medical files was a task nobody wanted and had been, consequently, one that I'd frequently wound up doing myself.

The heat and the long walk from Harriet's cottage and then to the Botanic Garden finally caught up to me. "I need to sit down. Just for a minute."

I moved toward a bench near the path under the shelter of some clearly labeled trees. I didn't care what they were called, though, just that their ancient branches blocked out the sun for the time being.

James agreed to stop with enough reluctance to let me know he wasn't happy about it, but I was so hot, I didn't care. Clearly he wasn't a man used to dawdling, but I supposed if you had made it in the New York publishing world, you wouldn't be known for your ability to relax. After a long pause, he sank down on the bench beside me.

The cool shade provided welcome relief. "I want to take it all in," I said, indicating the garden around me with one hand. The spire of Magdalen College towered in the foreground, and the drone of bees made me sleepy. Especially since I hadn't slept much the night before. Insomnia was apparently one of the prices I was paying for my current sins.

"It's nice," he said, glancing around.

Nice? His foot tapped the ground in a nervous pattern. Sitting still was definitely not his forte.

I had thought that an afternoon walk would give us a

chance to get to know each other. Despite the kiss I'd spurned the night before, I still couldn't accept that he was interested in me romantically. But the swarm of butterflies that invaded my stomach every time I saw him told me everything I needed to know about my own feelings.

He glanced around. "Are you ready to keep going?"

"In a moment." It had occurred to me, while I was catching my breath, that James was the very person to answer a question that had arisen during my walk back from Harriet's cottage.

"You know, I was wondering, what would happen if a famous author, somebody who's been dead a long time… I mean, what would happen if someone found a manuscript by a writer like that and it had never been published?"

"A famous author?" The corners of his mouth turned up into a smile. "Someone like, oh, Jane Austen, perhaps?"

I had to laugh. "Perhaps. But seriously, what would happen? If something like that turned up?"

He shrugged and shot me an inquisitive look. "I don't know what would happen in the academic world, but in the publishing business, well, it would be a feeding frenzy. Can you imagine the publicity?" He lifted a hand in the air. *"Lost Austen Novel."* He punctuated each word with a thrust of his hand. "It wouldn't even need to have a title to become an instant best seller."

"But who would get to publish it? Theoretically speaking," I added, trying to sound as casual as possible.

"Who would own the copyright, you mean?" He paused. "Whoever had legal possession of it."

"But I thought all of her novels were—what do you call it?—in the public domain."

"Yes. Because they were *published* novels. The copyright has long expired. But a new work? The owner and the publisher would stand to make a great deal of money." He laughed. "Theoretically speaking, of course. If a manuscript like that existed, someone would have come forward long before now. For financial reasons, if nothing else."

"Oh. I guess you're right." I let my gaze wander to a spire in the distance and thought about what James had said. I hadn't thought about the money angle at all. I knew what was concealed in my purse was rare and important, from a historical point of view, but it was clearly worth its weight in gold as well.

"I'm sorry. You want to keep moving, not talk about wild Jane Austen theories." I took pity on him and rose from the bench. "Let's go. I wouldn't mind something cold to drink."

"Good luck with that in this country." But he said it with a smile instead of a sneer. He was softening up a little bit.

We left the Botanic Garden and wandered up the road to Magdalen College. It sat along the High Street, somewhat apart from the other buildings, but it boasted the same golden medieval glow, dotted with red geraniums and emerald green patches of lawn. Some of those patches were tinged with brown after baking in the unusual summer heat.

Down the street toward the city center, we found a small shop, and I bought a room-temperature diet soda. We made our way back to the river near Christ Church and found a grassy spot underneath a sprawling tree. By then, the heat had finally taken a toll even on James's restlessness. I sat, legs tucked to the side in my best ladylike position. He stretched out full length and put his hands behind his head, as if he had all the time in the world. I wondered if he was always like this—either anxious or blasé, with no middle ground.

"Sorry about the garden," he said to the sky.

I took a swig of my Diet Coke. "It's okay." I paused. "Are *you* okay?"

"I guess I'm not used to being without my BlackBerry."

I glanced over at him. "So that's why you were twitching so much. CrackBerry withdrawal symptoms."

He sighed. "Yeah. Don't know what I was thinking, leaving it in my room. I thought it would be good for me."

We sat in silence for a while, the stillness of late afternoon wafting over us. A few people strolled in leisurely fashion along the river, and the occasional punt glided by. I envied the young women who trailed their hands in the water while their male admirers did the heavy work of poling the craft down the river. The arch of the trees, the tangy scent of the grass, the occasional breeze that wafted across the water created a haven of peace.

"We should do that," James said, nodding toward a punt as it passed.

"Looks like fun," I replied in an attempt to sound noncommittal. *Don't make too much of what he says*, I warned myself. I had never had an experience like this. I had never met a man and felt as if the earth were shifting position beneath my feet.

What about Neil? a voice in my head asked, but I decided to ignore it. That voice was annoying, and really, my love life wasn't any of its business.

To my surprise, in a few moments James was asleep. He snored, I thought with some amusement. Not a lot, but enough for it to be an imperfection. I need to find some imperfections in him so that I wouldn't feel quite so imperfect myself.

My own eyelids had grown heavy, and I was drifting off myself when my cell phone started to ring. I scrambled to open my purse, careful not to open it too wide, and dug around until I found the phone. The name and number on the display made me groan.

Neil.

"Hello?" I answered in a soft voice.

"Claire?"

"Hi, Neil." I pitched my voice low so that I wouldn't disturb James.

"Hey," he said. I did the mental calculation. It must have been late morning back in Kansas City. He was probably calling from work. "How's England?" he asked.

How's England? I had to bite my lip so I wouldn't laugh. Was this the same man who barely looked up from his copy of *Sports Illustrated* when I'd told him I was leaving the country?

The same man who couldn't drive me to the airport because the Royals had a home stand?

"Um, it's fine." I clutched the phone and tried to speak loud enough for Neil to hear me but not loud enough to wake up James. "What's wrong? Are Missy and the kids okay?" Panic squeezed my throat. I couldn't think of any reason Neil would call, unless...

"Everything's fine. Sorry, didn't mean to scare you."

"No, it's okay. I just wasn't expecting you to call."

There was a long pause. "I miss you," he finally blurted out. "When did you say you were coming home?"

"Saturday, Neil. I told you."

"I know, I know. Sorry."

I sat there in the grass, watching James, not knowing what to do. The sound of Neil's voice triggered a host of feelings I wasn't ready to deal with. Frustration. Affection. Confusion. Probably the last most of all.

"Did you need something?" I said and then realized that the question sounded snippy. I could almost hear Neil frowning at the other end of the line.

"I didn't think I had to need something for it to be okay to call."

"I didn't mean—"

"Missy said you were meeting a lot of new people."

What? My mind raced, trying to recall what I'd said to her on the phone the first night. Had I mentioned James?

I had. The memory hit me square in the stomach. What

had Missy said to Neil? She must have told him something about James. No way would he have placed a transatlantic call just to say hi.

"Yes, I am meeting people. Everyone's really nice. I've been to the botanical garden. And out to dinner at a very nice restaurant." Maybe it was mean, but I couldn't resist tweaking his nose just a little.

Was that a "harrumph" from Neil? I couldn't hear well enough to tell.

"Well, I just wanted to see how you were." He sounded as disgruntled as if I'd misplaced the remote during a big game.

"You're sweet to call." No reason why, if he was suffering from some pangs of jealousy, I couldn't let him stew in his own juices just a little. Maybe he wouldn't take me for granted quite so much when I got back home.

"Claire, is there anything you want to tell me?"

Subtlety certainly wasn't his strong point. "No. Not that I can think of."

He was silent for a long moment. "Okay, then. Well, good-bye."

"Good-bye, Neil. I'll see you on Saturday."

I ended the call and let the phone rest in my palm while I looked at James. What was Missy up to? I knew she thought Neil took me for granted, but since Missy pretty much did the same thing, it was like the pot calling the kettle black. Whatever she had said, it had at least motivated him to pick up the phone and call me.

For a few moments, I allowed myself to indulge in the satisfaction of having finally gotten Neil's attention. But being me, that satisfaction was quickly replaced by guilt. Not that I had done anything wrong, really. Going to dinner with James and enjoying our field trip to the Botanic Garden hardly qualified as romantic indiscretions. But not telling James about Neil...Well, on that score I would have to plead guilty.

I sat next to James on the grass for a long time as the sun sank lower in the sky. It was still full light, though, when at last I had to lean over and shake his arm to wake him.

"Dinner will be served soon."

He made a face. "The dining hall? Wouldn't you rather eat out again?"

My stomach gave a little leap at the question. More at the assumption, really, that we would share the meal together. I thought of the state of my finances and knew that I couldn't afford to pay my fair share at a restaurant like the Cherwell Boathouse, and I really couldn't, in good conscience, let him pay for dinner again. Not after Neil's phone call.

"Let's give the dining hall a try," I said. "Besides, we should be mingling with our classmates."

He sighed in mock resignation. "All right. You win."

"That remains to be seen," I muttered under my breath.

"What?"

"Nothing. Come on. We'd better hurry."

Since hurrying came naturally to him, we made it back to Christ Church in record time. Still, we were running late.

Fortunately, the only places left at the long tables in the dining hall were on either side of Martin Blakely.

"Delightful," he said when I asked if I could sit next to him. "Please, do join me."

James looked less than delighted at the prospect of Martin's company, but I decided to ignore him. If only I could ignore the manuscript pages still concealed in my purse. I had managed to get them and Martin in close proximity, but now I couldn't show them to him or ask his opinion without James overhearing.

The meal seemed to go on forever, but finally dessert and coffee were finished. I was making my excuses to return to my room when one of the porters materialized at my elbow.

"Miss Prescott, there's a package for you at the Porters' Lodge. You can retrieve it this evening if you go straightaway."

"For me? A package?" I felt my pulse quicken. "Yes, of course. I'll just—"

I made my excuses to James and Martin, rose from the table, and made a beeline for the door of the dining hall. My feet practically flew over the quad as I raced for the Porters' Lodge, because I had a feeling that I knew exactly who the package was from.

CHAPTER
TWELVE

 didn't know Harriet's handwriting, but I was sure that she was the sender. The package bore no postmark. I glanced over my shoulder, but no one had followed me from the Hall. With trembling fingers, I took the large manila envelope from the porter. I thanked him profusely and then scurried away, back across the quad and to the Meadow Building. The four flights of stairs seemed like eight, but at last I made it to the landing outside my door. I paused to catch my breath, and then I saw the note with my name on it taped to the dark wood.

If my heart could have beat any faster, it would have. As it was, my mouth simply went dry. I didn't recognize the handwriting. I reached out with a shaking hand and pulled the note from the door. My fingers trembled as I unfolded the piece of paper.

Miss Prescott,

If you would be so kind as to return the valuable item in your possession to Mrs. Dalrymple, I would be very much obliged.

Sincerely,

Gwendolyn Parrot

There was no reason that the wording of the note should frighten me, but it did. I fumbled with my key, unlocked the door, and stumbled into the room. I dumped my purse, the package, and the note on the bed and then collapsed in a heap next to them.

Before I could stop myself, I reached over, picked up the envelope, and ripped open the end. When I tilted it, the contents slid onto the bed. Familiar yellowed pages. Only not exactly familiar.

Attached to the first page was a note written in a spidery scrawl very different from the one that had been taped to my door.

Dearest Claire,

Found this shortly after Mrs. Parrot stomped away. Please keep it safe along with the rest. She's threatened to return tomorrow.

Best,

Harriet Dalrymple

Mrs. Parrot, whoever she was, was certainly the determined type. I looked at the pages, sprawled across the bed, and then reached for my purse to retrieve the others. With careful movements, I stacked them in their proper order. Well, at least as close to their proper order as I could get, since whole chapters were missing.

My curiosity, though, couldn't be denied for long. I made sure my door was locked, and then I reached for the stack of pages. I thumbed through them until I found the beginning of the newest section Harriet had sent. With a nervous glance at the door, I picked up the top page and began to read.

First Impressions
Chapter Five

Elizabeth had brought only one gown that might be deemed acceptable for a dinner party at Rosings. She had not expected to have the opportunity to wear much finery, even had she the means to obtain it. While Anne de Bourgh might require her company during the day, the sickly young woman became entirely her mother's property in the evenings.

I had to smile ruefully at that bit. I knew just how Elizabeth felt. Money had been so tight in the early years after my parents died that I often skipped church because I couldn't afford anything appropriate to wear. I knew, of course, that God didn't care about my attire, but I wasn't naive enough to think that other people didn't. So I'd told Missy I had to work overtime, dropped her off at the church doors, and spent the morning cleaning our small apartment or occasionally walking at a nearby park.

Elizabeth started in surprise when the footman came to inform her that her presence was expected downstairs. She dressed quickly but with care, her hair neat and her few pieces of jewelry left to their usual place in their pasteboard box. The unrelieved black of her gown, an unforgiving bombasine, did little to enhance her brown eyes or the healthy glow of her skin. Lady Catherine frowned upon Elizabeth's habit of a daily walk through the park, declaring that "Miss Bennet is far too tanned for fashion or good sense." But Elizabeth felt, privately of course, that Anne might benefit from just such fresh air and exercise.

A quarter hour later, neatly if somberly attired, Elizabeth approached the drawing room with more than her usual wariness.

When she reached the door, a liveried footman opened it for her, and Elizabeth entered with her head held as high as she dared. Lady Catherine and Anne had already claimed the sofa near the fire. The gentlemen were present, as was Mr. Humphreys, Lady Catherine's new curate. The rather whey-faced young man had arrived only two days before to take up his duties as well as his residence at the

Huntsford parsonage. Mr. Humphreys had the effect of making Elizabeth's cousin, Mr. Collins, appear a dashing romantic hero.

"There you are, Miss Bennet," Lady Catherine said as if she had been kept waiting for several hours rather than merely a fraction of that time. "We had begun to think you might never appear."

"My apologies, ma'am. I came as quickly as I could, once I knew I was wanted."

Out of the corner of her eye, Elizabeth saw a small smile light on Colonel Fitzwilliam's lips, but Mr. Darcy's impassive visage never wavered.

Lady Catherine sniffed but made no further comment, and turned her attention to the gentlemen instead.

"So, Darcy, you are to go to London when you leave us." Her tone evidenced her disapproval of his decision. She glanced at her daughter. "I should have liked to take Anne to town this spring to make her come-out, but her health will not permit it."

As if on cue, Anne coughed delicately into the lace handkerchief clutched in her thin fingers.

The section ended abruptly. I flipped the page over to see if there might be more on the reverse, but it was blank.

"Drat." But there were more pages in the stack in my lap. I picked up the next page to see where the narrative continued.

"*You must come as well, Miss Bennet,*" Mr. Humphreys said after the gentlemen had finished their port and rejoined the ladies in the drawing room. "*Miss de Bourgh, too, ma'am, if her health permits,*" he said with deference to Lady Catherine's judgment. "*I am as eager for female opinions as to the improvements for the house as I am for Mr. Darcy's advice about the stables.*"

While the young clergyman was as eager as his predecessor, he lacked the toad eating of Mr. Collins that had so nettled Elizabeth. Mr. Humphreys was awkward, but at least he was aware of his awkwardness.

"*I would be glad to accompany Miss de Bourgh,*" Elizabeth said carefully, "*if Lady Catherine deems her fit for the exercise.*"

The answer mollified Lady Catherine, who had bristled at the curate's initial request of Elizabeth.

"*I am sure if Darcy will offer Anne his arm, she will do very well.*" That was enough to establish the expedition with certainty.

Mr. Darcy's eyes darkened at his aunt's imperious command, but Elizabeth doubted anyone else of the party took notice. She owned herself surprised at the man's docility with regard to his aunt's dictates. He, who must be so accustomed to acting as lord and master, took her edicts rather well.

The engagement was set for the following afternoon.

Colonel Fitzwilliam said he would be glad to be of the party and would offer Miss Bennet his arm. Mr. Humphreys' disappointment at the addition of a rival for Elizabeth's attentions could not be concealed, for clearly he had envisioned the handsome Miss Bennet's hand resting atop the sleeve of his own coat. Nevertheless, the company was settled and the evening's conversation turned to other topics, directed firmly, to be sure, by Lady Catherine's preferences.

That was the end of it. I sighed with disappointment. Now there was yet another potential suitor for Elizabeth. The poor girl had to be as confused as I was.

The day's heat had yet to dissipate from my fourth-floor room. The one small window didn't provide much in the way of ventilation. Suddenly I was as restless as James had been earlier in the garden. I carefully slid the manuscript back into my purse, scooped up my room key, and letting myself out of the room, closed the door behind me. They would lock the gates soon, so I couldn't venture out of Christ Church, but perhaps I could find a quiet place to think. A quiet place with some semblance of an evening breeze.

The last light had faded from the sky, leaving the medieval buildings in shadow. I stepped carefully in the darkness toward the stairs to the dining hall. The quad lay just beyond. I didn't want to sit out there in the open, but perhaps I could find an accommodating nook or cranny somewhere.

I wandered toward the cathedral on the side of the quad opposite Tom Gate and the Porters' Lodge. To my surprise, it was still unlocked, so I slipped inside. The glow of candlelight relieved the dimness inside the church. I glanced around to see if I was alone.

I wasn't. To my surprise, I saw Martin Blakely sitting in a chair in one of the short rows against an outer wall.

"Martin?" I approached him almost on tiptoe. I hated to disturb the man at his prayers, but I really, really needed his help.

He glanced up and smiled when he saw me. "Claire." He nodded toward the chair next to him. "Would you care to join me?"

His formality, oddly enough, made me feel more comfortable.

"Thank you." I took the seat beside him and paused a moment to gather my thoughts.

We were quiet for several long moments. The peace of the cathedral washed over me. I hadn't been in very many churches since my parents' funeral, even when I had been able to afford something nice enough to attend. I'd avoided them, to tell the truth. Except for Missy and Phillip's wedding. My nieces' christenings. But other than that...

"I need your help," I said to Martin, deciding to cut to the chase. "But you'd have to promise me that you would never tell anyone about what I'm going to ask you."

His silvery eyebrows rose with intrigue. "A secret, is it?"

"Yes. And it's not my secret, which is why I need you to keep this confidential."

He nodded and rubbed his hands together in anticipation. "How may I assist you, my dear?"

My dear. It's what Harriet was always calling me, but given how I was about to betray her, I was anything but dear.

"I've come across something. A page of something related to Jane Austen. I need you to tell me if it might be authentic."

"Sounds mysterious."

"I don't mean for it to sound that way." I tried to keep the tremor out of my voice and my hands as I reached inside my purse for a manuscript page. "Can you promise me to hold this in confidence?"

His smile vanished then. "You're quite serious, aren't you?"

"Yes."

Now his eyebrows pulled toward the bridge of his nose in consternation. "Have you done anything…illegal?" he asked.

I shook my head. "No. Nothing like that."

Relief erased the lines around his eyes. "Good. Then I can promise you to keep this in confidence."

I could only hope that Martin would be as good as his word, because at that moment, his word was all I could depend on. The page had crumpled a bit at the edges in the confines of my bag. I pressed the wrinkles with the edge of my finger, and then I handed it to Martin.

"I was told that this was written by Austen herself, but I have no way of knowing. I thought you might be able to tell."

He took the page from me and then reached into the pocket

of his sports coat for a pair of reading glasses. He donned them and bent to examine the paper.

"Hmm." He made a musing noise at the back of his throat but was otherwise silent.

I sat quietly next to him and resisted the urge to fidget while he perused the page for what seemed a lifetime. I realized I was holding my breath and forced myself to exhale. It was all a hoax, of course. It must be. It had to be, not matter how sympathetic I found Harriet Dalrymple.

At long last, he lifted his eyes from the page, folded his reading glasses, and returned them to his coat pocket.

"If you don't mind my asking, where did you get this?"

I shook my head. "I'm afraid I can't tell you."

"I see."

"Is it real?" I asked quickly. "Can you tell?"

I was on pins and needles as I waited for his answer. So much depended on his assessment. If the manuscript was a fake, it was just another lie in a string of them that had comprised my Oxford experience. But if it were real...Well, if it were real, that changed everything, didn't it?

Martin handed the paper back to me. "Is there more or just this page?"

I knew then what his answer was.

"There's more," I said and swallowed heavily. "Quite a bit more, although I don't think all of it is intact."

He shook his head, disbelief and ruefulness mingling on his face. "I'd give a great deal to see it," he said with a tight smile.

"I'm afraid it's not mine to share," I said. "I'm breaking my word by showing this to you."

"Your word?" He looked even more intrigued than when I'd shown him the page. "So you really have been sworn to secrecy?"

I nodded.

His gaze locked with mine. "Does the name Formidables mean anything to you?" he asked.

I gasped. I couldn't help it. "How did you know—"

He laughed but looked dismayed. "I didn't know. Not until I saw your face just now. But I've long suspected. And hoped. I told you there were secrets to be uncovered in Oxford."

"What do you know about them?" Maybe I was betraying Harriet more than I already had, but the whole thing had become so incredibly complicated, and I needed an ally. I couldn't sense any malice in Martin, any reason that he might be a threat to Harriet.

He tapped the page where it lay in my lap. The gesture reminded me of Harriet. "I've only heard rumors, I'm afraid. That they are a group conceived by Austen's sister, Cassandra, who said that she burned all of Austen's correspondence and other personal papers. Some scholars have speculated that she might not have been telling the truth. That perhaps she was protecting her sister."

"Why would it matter if Jane Austen's letters came to light? Or an early manuscript, like this?"

Martin rubbed his chin. "A woman's reputation is a delicate

thing. Even the reputation of a literary genius. Or perhaps especially the reputation of a literary genius."

"So Cassandra thought the letters and early manuscripts would make her sister look bad?"

Martin shrugged. "People often make strange choices when loved ones die. Jane Austen's sister would not have been the first person to make unorthodox decisions in the midst of grief."

"But why would anyone think less of her because this early version of *Pride and Prejudice* came to light?"

"From what you've shown me, it doesn't have the full genius of her later work. We all choose what of ourselves we want to present to the world," he said. "Would Jane Austen have been any different?"

I bit my lip, because I understood that reality all too well. I'd spent most of my adult life convincing people that I was competent, in charge, unafraid, when in fact, I'd been struggling, desperate, terrified. I couldn't afford to let people see the real me, the Claire who cried at night for her mother and father as if she were a child of ten, not a woman of eighteen. Or twenty-five. Or even thirty-one, to own the truth.

"So you think she was afraid that people would value her work less if they knew more about her? If they could read her early efforts?"

"Well, not every early effort, obviously. We have some of those. *Lady Susan*, the epistolary novel she wrote early on. And her *Juvenalia*, of course. But those writings were obviously the work of a child. No, there must have been something about this manuscript in particular that she didn't want people to know. Many things changed in her life in the ten years between the two drafts, after all."

"But why didn't she destroy it herself?"

"It's a rare author who could," Martin said.

"I suppose so." I couldn't imagine setting fire to something I'd worked so hard on, although in the past few weeks, I'd done a pretty good job of annihilating the life I'd spent more than a decade constructing.

"How much of this have you read?" He nodded toward the page in my lap.

"Just a few sections. Enough to know that it's very different from the novel we read for the seminar."

I answered Martin, but my mind was focusing on what he'd said about people making unorthodox choices in the face of grief. After my parents died in the car accident, everyone around me had insisted that I was far too young to take care of Missy. They had argued with me, tempted me, tried to persuade me. But I'd made my own unorthodox decision during my time of enormous grief. And I had never regretted it.

Never, until now, the voice in my head whispered.

"So you think this is the real thing?" I asked, trying to redirect my thoughts away from the perilous course they had taken. "A lost Austen manuscript?"

Martin rose from his chair. "It would appear so. I can only

say how much I envy you, Claire. You must have done something to earn the trust of one of these Formidables."

I blushed with shame. "And taken very little time to betray it."

He reached out and patted my shoulder. "It's quite a dilemma, isn't it? To be offered something so spectacular, but only on promise of secrecy? I'm sure I'd want to give it to the university where I taught. Any American school would give their eyeteeth for something like this."

I stood up, too, and moved into the aisle. Martin followed, and we turned toward the entrance of the cathedral. "What would you do if you were me?" I asked.

He couldn't help but chuckle. "There aren't many holy grails left in the world these days. It's a shame to keep one hidden if you find it."

We stepped through the door onto the wide, paved walkway on Tom Quad.

"The thing I have learned in my years of study," he said, "is that 'truth will out,' as they say. The question is usually one of timing, not of eventuality."

"Huh?"

He leaned forward and pressed a kiss to my cheek. "Follow your heart, my dear," he said, before stepping back and winking at me. "That's what Jane Austen would tell you, I would imagine."

Follow my heart? I wasn't sure I even had one anymore.

"I'll try. And thank you." I reached out my hand, and he shook it.

"Good luck," he said. "I have a feeling you're going to need it."

"Thanks." I wasn't sure whether his words were a blessing or a curse.

"And if you happen to get your hands on the whole manuscript, I wouldn't mind a peek at it," Martin added with a wink. "Strictly in confidence, of course."

I laughed, and he turned to walk toward the far side of the quad, away from the dining hall behind us. The night breeze had finally arrived, and I stood outside the cathedral, letting the cool air soothe my confusion and my battered heart.

If that poor pathetic organ was going to serve as my compass, it was going to need all the help it could get.

s it turned out, Martin and I weren't the only ones prowling the environs of Christ Church that night. The gates would close soon, at ten o'clock, but as I walked toward the dining hall, its Gothic arches and high windows silhouetted against the dark sky, I saw someone coming toward me.

James.

"I think we're destined to keep running into each other," he said with his customary stiffness but also a hint of a smile. "I thought you'd gone to your room for the night."

"I thought I had too. Where are you headed?" I was curious to know where he had been and if he had been looking for me specifically, but I didn't ask. I didn't have to.

He nodded toward the passageway behind him. "I was sitting in the Master's Garden, but they roll up the sidewalks pretty early around here. Time to turn in, I guess."

"Yeah. I guess so." Only I didn't want to go back to my room. Or, more to the point, I didn't want to be alone. Not anymore.

"Do you want to sit down for a moment?" he asked, and my heart executed a funny little leap. I wished it would quit doing that whenever I saw him or talked to him.

"Sure."

He glanced around. "Hmm…"

"There's not really anywhere to sit, is there?" I knew that the Junior Commons, along with the gate, had been locked up. And the Master's Garden would have been too. We could have perched on the edge of the quad, but I didn't want to talk to James in full view of God and everyone.

He eyed the stairs behind us that led to the dining hall, two short flights with a wide landing in the middle. "Not very fancy, but…"

James sank down onto a step, which was shadowed by the stone balustrade, and I followed his lead so that we were tucked away from sight, but with a good view of the quad. The tower above the cathedral was now lit up against the night, and floodlights cast eerie shadows against the medieval architecture.

"Was your package important?" James asked. "You took off like a shot after dinner."

"Sorry."

"It wasn't bad news or anything? Nothing to do with a patient?"

I looked at him in confusion for a moment and then

remembered my charade. I shook my head. His shoulder was just inches from mine, and I was aware of every part of him, even though we weren't touching anywhere. I was as miserable and as happy as I had ever been in my life.

How had it come to this? Achingly close to the kind of man I'd always thought out of my reach, in a place I'd never thought I'd actually see, embroiled in a plot straight out of a movie. I'd never felt lonelier and wished suddenly for Missy and my nieces and even Phillip, who was usually grateful to see me but never really glad.

That thought brought me up short. Was it true? Was that how my brother-in-law felt about me? Here, against the timeless backdrop of Christ Church, I could feel the accuracy of the observation that I'd buried, probably a long time ago, so I wouldn't have to acknowledge it. Maybe Phillip's running joke about acquiring two wives for the price of one wasn't really that funny to him.

"You're very quiet," James said after a long silence.

I tried to smile but couldn't. "You're not exactly a chatterbox yourself."

He lifted a hand toward the rest of Christ Church, a view partially blocked by the stone sides of the staircase. "Something about this place lends itself to contemplation," he said.

"Unfortunately, I think you're right."

He laughed then, soft and low, and I felt another tingle of awareness ripple through me. I hadn't expected this at all. Hadn't planned for it in any way. But here I was, for whatever reason. Was I hoping for a great romance? Or was I merely looking for an escape from the mess I had made of my life?

He reached over and took my hand. I jumped at the contact, and he started to pull away, but I gripped his hand tightly. "Sorry." The word sounded breathless. Probably because it was.

"Claire—"

"Yes?"

"Do you believe in fate?"

A knot formed in my throat, thick and hard. "No. I don't, actually." I couldn't afford to believe in it, but I didn't tell James that. No, the only thing I believed in was the randomness of life. Tragic, random events that defined one's life and shaped one's character.

Even though it was dark, I could tell he was smiling. "A true empirical scientist, hmm?" He squeezed my hand. "I suppose they drill that kind of thing into your head in medical school."

"What about the business world? Shouldn't you be as logical as a Vulcan in order to succeed?"

"Touché."

He was quiet then for a long time, and it was enough for me simply to sit there on the hard stone of the dining-hall stairs, his hand wrapped warmly around mine. I couldn't remember the last time anyone over the age of seven had held my hand. I couldn't remember Neil ever having done so.

The bell in Tom Tower began to chime the hour. Ten o'clock. I felt like Cinderella at the ball, as if at any moment, the magic might end. Maybe the wisest course was to end it myself. Nothing could come of my infatuation with James. Even if he was attracted to me, what we felt was simply the grown-up version of a summer-camp romance. It couldn't be worth throwing away my relationship with Neil.

"I'd better head for bed," I said, pulling my hand free of his. "I have to present my sister's paper in the morning." In the twists and turns of the day, I'd almost forgotten.

"I'll walk you home," he said with a touch of good-humored irony in his voice.

We stood up and took the shorter route beneath the stairs toward the Meadow Building. And then, unexpectedly, he pulled me into the shadow of the staircase.

"I wasn't expecting this," he said, sounding almost apologetic. "I didn't plan—"

And then I felt his lips on mine. In the darkness, I hadn't seen them coming. But they were there, and they were warm, warmer than the night, and soft and firm at the same time. I'd been waiting for that kiss, wanting that kiss since the moment I saw him in the doorway of the Junior Common Room, and now it had finally happened.

He was good. I had to give him that. As abrupt as his manner sometimes was, his kissing wasn't. Slow. Thorough. Thrilling. I should have been ashamed and distraught and kicking myself from one end of Oxford to the other for what I was doing to Neil. But instead I just kept kissing James until he groaned and set me away from him.

"Stop." His voice was raspy.

"I…" My vocal chords refused to cooperate. I paused to clear my throat. "I didn't start it," I choked out eventually.

That quieted him for a long moment. "No. You didn't."

I could feel frustration and something darker emanating from him in waves. And then I wondered why he seemed so upset about a kiss between two people who had spent as much time together as we had in the past few days. He didn't know about Neil, so I figured it couldn't be that.

"It's late." I took a step backward and wished that I could see his face in the darkness. If I could just see his expression, I'd know better how to handle such a moment. "Don't worry about it. It's no big deal." Even though my breath still rattled in my chest from the intensity of that kiss.

"Claire, I don't want to give you the wrong impression…"

He was dumping me.

"The only impression you were giving me was with your tongue," I shot back, unable to keep the irritation from my voice. I knew that I was beneath him, but he shouldn't have been thinking that. Not when I'd told so many lies to put myself up on his level. He should have been on his knees, thanking the heavens that I so much as noticed him. Not telling me what big a mistake it had been to kiss me.

"Claire—"

"I think it's time to call it a night." I spun on my heel and prayed I wouldn't walk straight into a wall in the darkness.

Where was the moon when you needed it? "I'll see you around tomorrow."

"Let me ex—"

"Good night," I called over my shoulder.

I found the other opening beneath the stairs that led to the Meadow Building. His room was in the opposite direction. If I heard any footsteps behind me, it meant he was coming after me. I listened for them, even though I begged myself not to, but there were no footsteps except for mine.

I hurried across the gravel courtyard and made a beeline for the door of my staircase. I felt every one of those flights of stairs in my legs, and by the time I reached the top, I didn't have enough breath left in my lungs to cry the tears that wanted to escape.

Happy endings were for other people. I'd known that since I was eighteen years old. I scrambled to the top of the stairs and then stopped short.

The door to my room stood open, and inside I could see my belongings flung wildly around the room.

t was sometime after midnight before the security officers and other assorted Christ Church employees finished looking over the chaos in my room and taking their reports. Not that I slept much after that. I kept double-checking the lock on the door and wondering which of the likely candidates had ransacked my room in search of the manuscript. Mrs. Parrot? Eleanor? Or someone else entirely?

I skipped breakfast in the Hall the next morning. I would have done anything to avoid seeing James, even sacrifice my morning's ration of caffeine. While everyone else was filling up on eggs, toast, and black pudding—well, maybe not the black pudding—I darted across the quad like a fugitive from justice and arrived at the seminar room half an hour before we were due to start, the manuscript pages still tucked safely in my purse.

Given the state of my luck, I wasn't surprised to find Eleanor already there.

"Good morning." I nodded, stifling a groan, and then went to sit in the farthest chair possible.

Without looking up, I reached into my bag and pulled out the manila folder that held Missy's paper. I flipped it open and pretended to read, pretended to be engrossed, actually, but the truth was that I couldn't make any sense of the words on the page. They might as well have been in Sanskrit, for all the sense they made to me.

"Claire, I'm glad you're here early," Eleanor said.

I still didn't look up until I heard her rise from her chair and move toward me. I had a brief mental image of frying pans and fires, with me leaping back and forth between them, before Eleanor settled stiffly into the chair next to me.

"Yes?" I decided to play innocent.

"I meant it, Claire, when I asked you to leave my mother alone."

"I'm not doing anything to hurt her," I said, but I couldn't help the defensive tone in my voice. "She's a very nice lady."

"You'll only agitate her by listening to all her mad theories," Eleanor snapped.

"You don't believe her, then?" I wondered that her own daughter hadn't bothered to do as much as I had, asking Martin Blakely or someone like him to pass judgment on at least a portion of the manuscript. Besides, Eleanor's attitude didn't mesh with what Harriet had told me about her daughter's desire to get her hands on the manuscript.

Eleanor's face tightened and then drooped into lines of

dismay. "She ought to give up the cottage and move to a facility where she can receive proper care. But no, she won't budge. She has to be near the college."

I studied Eleanor's face, trying to figure out whether she was lying.

"Maybe she just wants to be near you?" I barely spoke the words above a whisper, but they sounded loud in my own ears.

Eleanor's head snapped up, and her spine straightened. "My relationship with my mother is none of your affair."

"I know. You're right." After all, who was I to be giving her, or anyone, advice about how to conduct herself when it came to family dynamics? "It's only that, well, she seems more lonely than demen…" I couldn't bring myself to say the word.

"She has dementia," Eleanor protested. "The doctors confirmed it."

"Maybe she does. But she's as lucid as most people I've ever met. Most of the time, anyway." Having lost my mother at such an early age, I couldn't understand Eleanor's attitude. I would have given anything to have my mother living in a picturesque cottage up the road. Or a hovel, for that matter. The living part, not the quality of the house, was the key factor. "What if you're wrong about her theories?"

Eleanor shook her head. "See her if you must, Claire, but please remember that in a few days, you'll be gone and I'll be left here to console her."

"To console her?"

"She'll be devastated when you leave. She so rarely finds someone who will listen to her ravings."

You could listen to them. I pressed my lips together to keep from vocalizing the thought. Whatever stood between Harriet and Eleanor, it wasn't something I could fix. Not in the space of a few days. Not when my own life was such a mess.

"I'm sorry if she'll be upset. I'll do my best to help her understand."

"*Hmmph.*" Eleanor's head lifted in a regal manner. "I can't forbid you, obviously. But I would have thought you would respect my wishes."

I would have thought so too, but that was before I'd thrown my moral code to the wind and embarked on my current course of dishonesty and deviousness.

"I'm sorry, Eleanor."

"Not sorry enough." She glanced at her watch. "The others will be here in a moment. I want you to promise me that you won't see my mother again."

I swallowed hard. "I can't." The words were almost a squeak. "I have to return something to her."

She shook her head. "You can give it to me. I'll see that it's returned to my mother."

I shook my head. "I can't."

Eleanor's jaw hardened, as did her eyes. "I must warn you—"

Footsteps echoed on the staircase and in the hallway just

outside the door. I said a silent prayer of thanksgiving for whoever had decided to show up early that morning.

My gratitude didn't last long. James appeared in the doorway, scowling at me. I bristled and sat up straighter. Why
should he be scowling at me? He was the one who had spurned
me the night before.

Spurned. I really had been reading too much Jane Austen.

"Good morning," he said stiffly and went to sit close to
Eleanor.

"Morning." I retrieved the folder containing Missy's paper
and buried my nose in it so I wouldn't have to look at him.

Eleanor's head bobbed up, a pointer who scented tension
as if it were her quarry. "Hello, James. You're early as well."
Then her eyes narrowed, and she looked from me to James and
then back again. "Is everything all right?"

I would rather have been tortured than admit to Eleanor
Gibbons that I was anything less than perfect.

"Everything's fine." The words gushed out like water from
a hydrant. "Perfect, in fact. Sheer bliss."

James gave me an odd look, and I thought I saw Eleanor
rolling her eyes.

"I'll have you go first, then, Claire. Are you prepared?"

Fear coalesced into a ball in my stomach. "Sure." I shifted in
my chair and took deep breaths. Lots and lots of deep breaths.

"The Role of Sisterhood in *Pride and Prejudice*." It had
seemed rather straightforward up until now. Jane was Lizzie's
good sister. The other three were bad. Or at least highly

problematic. Darcy's sister Georgiana, who'd committed a youthful indiscretion, was a bit of a mixed bag. Nothing earth shattering.

Why, then, did I feel so uneasy?

I crumpled the folder between my fingers as the three of us waited in uncomfortable silence for the rest of the group to arrive. James glowered at the empty bookshelf across from him and gave no more notice of me than he would to a potted plant. Eleanor was reading something, probably a handbook on how to rid yourself of unwanted pests who wouldn't leave your aging mother alone. Somewhere a clock ticked ominously and made me feel like a condemned prisoner.

At last, though, the others arrived. Martin led them in like the grand marshal of a parade, Olga towering behind him and the New Zealand ladies laughing and smiling at his witticisms. The cardiologist looked slightly more relaxed now that he'd gotten over the hurdle of presenting. I could only hope that I would feel the same in the very near future.

"So, then, shall we begin?" Eleanor looked particularly severe in a black turtleneck and a sensible tweed skirt.

I had no idea how she withstood all that wool. I was melting in my sleeveless dress and sandals. Still, I was the one with perspiration beading my brow, while she looked as cool as a cucumber. A very intimidating cucumber who also happened to be rather displeased with me.

"Claire?" She smiled at me, only it wasn't really a smile at all. "Why don't you begin?"

"Sure." I straightened in my chair and opened the folder in my lap. Then I looked around the group and gave them a smile of my own, one even less authentic than Eleanor's.

"As some of you know, my sister couldn't be here, so I'm presenting the paper on her behalf."

Martin nodded encouragingly and winked at me. The New Zealand ladies made slight cooing noises of encouragement, and Olga sat up straight, pen poised above her notepad. The cardiologist's eyelids were drooping, so I decided to look at him while I was speaking.

"*Pride and Prejudice* gives Austen the ideal vehicle to examine the gift, and the curse, of sisterhood," I began, my voice wavering. I stopped, cleared my throat, and then forged ahead. "While the relationship between Jane and Elizabeth has long been thought to present the apex of the sisterly bond…" *Apex of the sisterly bond?* I wasn't even sure what that meant. "…Elizabeth's three younger sisters provide a substantial threat to the older pair achieving their dreams of marriage." So far, so good. "And yet," I read, "one must ask whether the well-intentioned Elizabeth in fact proves to be a significant obstacle in her own right to her sister Jane's happiness."

Huh? Now that I was reading Missy's words aloud, they seemed different than when I'd read them on the plane.

"Jane and Bingley do secure one another's affections in the end, but Elizabeth's attempts to 'help' her sister"—why was the word *help* in quotation marks?—"actually hinder Jane's ability to craft her own happy ending."

Hinder? How was helping someone hindering them? And suddenly I realized that Missy wasn't talking about Jane and Elizabeth Bennet at all. No, she was clearly talking about Missy and Claire Prescott, whether she realized it or not. The ball of fear in my stomach crawled up into my throat and lodged near my vocal chords. I sat in silence for several long moments and tried to remember to breathe. Deeply. Or, barring that, at all.

After a long moment, I found my voice again. "While Elizabeth appears to be working for Jane's good, her actions undermine Jane's best interests. For example, Elizabeth's tromp through the fields to visit her sister when she is ill at Netherfield Park lowers Jane's standing in the eyes of Mr. Bingley's sisters and his best friend, Mr. Darcy."

Undermine? Was she kidding with this?

I continued to read, but I hardly paid attention anymore. Missy's meaning was quite clear. While generations of readers might have thought Elizabeth Bennet a stellar sister who loved and supported Jane, Missy took exception to that interpretation. No, to Missy, Elizabeth Bennet was the cause of Jane's difficulties, not her solace in them. Her sister's helpfulness was, in fact, the very evil that kept Jane from making her feelings known to Mr. Bingley and, thus, attaching him and securing her future as well as her family's.

"Elizabeth Bennet is hardly worthy of a hero like Mr. Darcy," I read, heat rising in my cheeks.

Was that how Missy felt about me? My hands trembled where they clutched the edges of the paper. Years of sacrifice and hard work, and for what? So that my sister could believe that I had, in fact, hindered her own quest for happiness? That I didn't deserve any of my own?

I tried to keep my voice from shaking as I approached the end of the paper, but I was only partially successful. Should I feel betrayed? Indignant? I didn't know. All I did know was that I was devastated.

"Jane Austen understood all too well from personal experience that sisterly devotion could easily cross into dependence, and while both Jane and Lizzie achieve their dream of a love match, the happy ending arrives in spite of, rather than due to, Elizabeth's actions."

I finished the last page and set it in my lap with a carefully controlled motion. I glanced from one face to the next, but the others simply smiled or nodded in bland agreement.

"An interesting notion," Eleanor said. Her look was neither bland nor smiling. In fact, she looked pleased, in a rather cross sort of way. "Elizabeth as villainess. I've not heard that one before."

"Yes, well, my sister does tend to have a rather...unique take on things." I closed the folder and crossed my hands on top of it, but it was like closing the lid to Pandora's box long after its evils had escaped.

"I'd never quite considered that before," Rosie said in her soft New Zealand accent. "Still, I'm not sure I can accept that Elizabeth did more harm than good. She certainly intended the best for her sisters. All of them, not just Jane."

"You know what they say about the road to hell," said the cardiologist with a chuckle.

"So Elizabeth should have conformed more to the standards of her day?" Olga asked the group in general, her tone slightly indignant. "She should have succumbed to the demands of patriarchy and proved a compliant, mousy sister?" Her heavily plucked eyebrows formed arches that would have been at home in the Hall. She looked at me. "What do you think of your sister's thesis?"

Any words that I might have said couldn't escape past the knot in my throat. What did I think of Missy's point of view? The problem was that I could understand it all too well. I could say that since my arrival in England, I had begun to see my own behavior over the past decade in a different light. What I thought was that Missy might, in fact, have a point. And that thought, that admission, made me want to cry.

But I wasn't about to cry in front of these people, especially not in front of James or Eleanor.

"I'm merely the messenger," I said with the slightest of smiles. It was all I could manage to produce. I forced my voice not to tremble. "I learned long ago not to take responsibility for my sister." It was the biggest lie I had told since I'd arrived on English soil. I'd spent the whole of my adult life taking responsibility for everything to do with Missy. And now I was being told, albeit indirectly and while I was an ocean away, that my efforts had not been appreciated. Not in the least.

"So what do the rest of you think?" Eleanor waded into

the silence that followed my disclaimer. "Was Elizabeth a good sister or a bad one?"

I could have sworn she had a gleam in her eye, as if she perfectly understood the reason for my distress, but surely I was imagining it. She didn't know anything about Missy or anything about me, other than that I was noncompliant when it came to her request that I leave her mother alone.

Louise patted Rosie's knee next to her. "Sisters are rather more complicated than that, though, aren't they? Austen understands that thoroughly. Look at those Bennet girls. They're all unique, as are their relationships with one another. Really, I think the problem here is down to Mr. Bingley's sisters. They do the most damage to his prospects for happiness. And Jane Bennet's." Louise smiled at me, an offering of consolation and support.

Martin nodded. "An excellent point. And I, for one, think it's a bit far-fetched to blame Elizabeth for Jane's difficulties. Austen makes it clear that Jane guards her feelings too closely. If she had been more open toward Bingley, she would have attached him at the beginning."

"And thus spared all of us the next several hundred pages," said James.

I gaped at him, and a sudden wave of color washed his cheeks. Clearly he'd not meant to speak the words aloud.

Olga scribbled something furiously in her notebook, the cardiologist looked amused, and Eleanor gave a harrumphing noise.

"Yes, well, there are those of us who find the next several hundred pages quite fascinating." She turned away from James and addressed a comment to Martin, but I didn't hear what she said.

From his seat several chairs away, James was looking at me, a glint of laughter in his eyes just as there had been on that first day when our gazes had met and I'd felt the connection from one end of my body to the other.

Only it was too late now. James had made his feelings clear. I broke eye contact and turned my attention back to Eleanor. Well, not my attention exactly, but at least my gaze. The conversation had moved on into a more general discussion, and I made every effort to nod and look thoughtful in the right places.

Martin, bless him, carried the conversational ball with aplomb, and sooner than I could have hoped, the discussion time for Missy's paper ended. Eleanor declared a tea interval before the next presentation, and I practically leaped from my chair, brushing past the others to escape to the restroom.

Airing my family's dirty linen, even in such an oblique way, called for a strategic retreat and some significant nursing of my wounds.

CHAPTER
FIFTEEN

Since James wasn't ready yet to present and Martin asked to be the last to share his paper, we spent the remainder of the morning debating some of the finer points of *Pride and Prejudice*, such as whether Wickham was inherently evil or whether the loss of his father had scarred him so much that he couldn't behave properly. The men tended to take the first view, and the women the second.

As soon as Eleanor dismissed us for lunch, I hurried from the seminar room before James could catch up with me. I wasn't about to turn up at the Hall for the noon meal, not when his rejection the night before still stung so fiercely. And especially not when I'd just put myself through the emotional wringer while presenting what should have been a routine paper.

I made it out Tom Gate and down the street before anyone could stop me. After the previous night's break-in, I was eager to check on Harriet. To my relief, she answered the door almost as soon as I knocked.

"More tea, of course," she said as she led me into the sitting room. "You look as if you could do with the contents of the entire pot."

I simply nodded my agreement.

While she stepped out to make the tea, I retrieved the manuscript from my bag and laid it on the table next to the sofa. I'd become accustomed to the slightly stale smell of old books, the troublesome broken springs in the cushion beneath me, and the warmth of the cottage, which comforted rather than stifled. My eyelids began to droop, and the next thing I knew, Harriet was sliding the tea tray on the low table in front of me.

"Needed a bit of a sleep, did you? Well, I expect that's the jet lag. And the stress, of course."

"Of course. Look, Harriet, about yesterday—"

"You've read what I sent to you last evening?"

I nodded and tried to look composed, but I was still ashamed. "Harriet, I'm very sorry, but I've broken your confidence. I know you asked me not to—"

She froze. "You've shown the manuscript to someone else?"

I took a sip of the steaming hot tea. "Only one page to Martin Blakely, and he's sworn to secrecy. Nothing's proven one way or the other, but Martin certainly thought it looked authentic."

Harriet looked troubled. "Of course it's authentic."

"I just needed to be sure—"

"Because you didn't believe me." Harriet's shoulders drooped.

"It's not that I didn't believe you."

"No. It's just that I'm an old woman who's going daft."

Her eyes darkened and grew moist, and I felt as if I'd kicked a puppy.

"Harriet, have you found any more of the manuscript?" I asked gently.

"Yes." She took a deep breath and seemed to compose herself. "I found another bit when I was clearing out the linen cupboard at the top of the stairs."

The linen cupboard at the top of the stairs? Well, of course that's where one would find precious bits of a lost Austen manuscript. I took another sip of tea so that I could hide my expression. Now I couldn't even bring myself to tell her about the break-in.

Harriet wasn't paying attention to me, though. She rose from her perch, disappeared into the hallway, and then returned in a mere moment with a fresh stack of pages—well, if one could call two-hundred-year-old paper fresh.

"Here they are." She put the pages in my lap, but she still looked distressed. "I'm lucky to find all these bits in order. Usually it's willy-nilly."

"Thank you." I laid a hand on her arm. "Thank you for sharing this with me." I knew she was disappointed in me, but for whatever reason, she was still willing to trust me to read more of her treasure, and I was humbled by her trust.

"I'll just leave you to it, then." Harriet rose from the sofa looking more like her usual self. "That cupboard won't clean itself out." She gave me a look that mingled disappointment and hope. "Let me know if you want more tea." And once more she slipped from the room, leaving me alone with the precious pages.

First Impressions

Chapter Ten

As it happened, Elizabeth was only too glad of Colonel Fitzwilliam's company when the time came to visit Huntsford parsonage. Mr. Humphreys greeted the carriage at the gate and offered Miss de Bourgh his arm, an action that displeased Lady Catherine and left Elizabeth standing alone until Mr. Darcy and Colonel Fitzwilliam arrived on horseback a few moments later. Shortly thereafter Elizabeth found herself tête-à-tête with the colonel.

All the members of the party, even Miss de Bourgh, were engaged to stroll about the garden and toward the stables, which though not covering a great distance, still gave Elizabeth a quarter hour to extract what information she could from the colonel about his cousin.

"Do you often visit Rosings, Colonel?" she said as they walked behind the others. Mr. Humphreys was speaking with rapturous delight about the changes he had made to the kitchen garden, and while the space was ample and the plants well tended, Elizabeth could hear

Lady Catherine's imperious commands as to necessary, and indeed immediate, improvements.

"We visit our aunt three or four times a year," the colonel said, casting a glance in that estimable personage's direction. By this time, Lady Catherine had succeeded in transferring Anne's escort from Mr. Humphreys to Mr. Darcy.

"And is their engagement of longstanding?" Elizabeth asked with a nod toward the couple, even as she despised herself for the contrived artlessness of her question.

That much I remembered from the final version of *Pride and Prejudice*. Darcy and Anne were supposed to get married, if their mothers had their way. Clearly, Lady Catherine's designs on Darcy had survived Austen's rewrite.

The colonel paused. "Engagement? I am aware of no formal pledge, Miss Bennet. Only an understanding between my aunt and Darcy's mother. A sisterly inclination, but nothing more."

Indeed? Hope sprang to life in Elizabeth's breast. If there were no formal engagement…And then she stopped, quite literally in the midst of the path, a flush heating her face and neck.

So Elizabeth had fallen for Darcy rather early on in this version.

"Miss Bennet? Are you unwell?" The colonel drew her off the path to a plain wooden bench beneath the shelter of a beech tree. "Shall I fetch you a glass of water? Or some wine?"

"No, no. I am quite well, Colonel. I am sorry to inconvenience you. Pray, join the others and leave me here to collect myself. I really am quite well, I assure you."

But the colonel would not dream of leaving her unattended no matter how Elizabeth might urge him to withdraw. Though her inquiry had been slight and almost innocent, she recognized in her heart the seeds of hope. Mr. Darcy's strange attentions to her over the last week could only be ascribed to boredom. Certainly she should not make assumptions simply because he so often turned up just as she was setting off for her daily turn about the park, or because he offered to turn the pages of her music when Lady Catherine commanded her to the pianoforte in the evenings. And yet here she was, shamelessly culling information from Colonel Fitzwilliam.

"You said when we met that you had been too long from your regiment." She vowed to fix her attention on the colonel and keep her eyes from following the tall figure moving toward the stables. "Do you plan to return to duty soon, then, sir?" She knew from Lady Catherine's boasts that the colonel had fought valiantly against the French.

He grimaced. "I am to sell out, Miss Bennet, at the end of the summer. So, no, I am not to rejoin my regiment."

"*You sound as if you regret the choice, sir.*"

His weather-beaten face grew tight. "*I do, Miss Bennet. Indeed, I do. But my father has made me an offer I cannot refuse.*"

"*What sort of offer, sir?*"

"*A small but handsome property that adjoins our family pile. The rents are modest but not insignificant, and I may enjoy the life of a gentleman after all these years of following the drum.*"

It sounded rather like Longbourn, which caused her heart to twist in her breast. "*And will you miss soldiering?*"

"*I will. I will indeed, Miss Bennet.*" *He was no older than his cousin, she surmised, and yet he seemed to have an air of experience that even the formidable Mr. Darcy did not possess. Yet his manner was softened by something. A hint of weariness, perhaps?*

"*But you will be glad to settle in one place, surely?*"

He smiled. "*It is human nature, I suppose, to always want what we do not have. For many years I longed for a home and hearth of my own. And now that I am to be a settled gentleman, I find that I've still a great deal of the soldier in me.*"

"*Change is always difficult.*" *Elizabeth laid a hand on the sleeve of his coat.* "*Time will aid you in coming to terms with your situation.*"

He looked up, and his gaze held hers. "*Do you speak from experience, Miss Bennet? Pardon my directness, but*

I wonder at your optimism." He paused. "I mean, given your situation. I do not mean to speak ill of my aunt, but—"

Elizabeth shook her head. "A woman's ability to adapt must serve me in my circumstances," she said, regret and longing in her voice, she was sure. "Men have the means to be independent. You do not need to learn acceptance in the same way we must." Sudden tears swam in her eyes, and she turned her face from him. Of all things, she did not want his pity. Or anyone's, for that matter.

"Miss Bennet—" He took her hand from his sleeve and held it in his, and Elizabeth closed her eyes at the touch.

He was a man accustomed to protecting king and country. No doubt when he chose to take a wife, he would protect her as well. If only his cousin were more like him. She refused to think of what had happened the evening before, at the top of the stairs. She refused to think of Mr. Darcy's eyes, or the way she had felt when he had kissed her.

Kissed her? My mouth dropped open in astonishment, and I was very sorry that Harriet hadn't found that particular section of the manuscript.

"I think the others have returned to the house," Elizabeth said, shaking off her melancholy and turning

her attention to the moment. "They will be expecting us. I believe Mr. Humphreys mentioned that his housekeeper possesses a dab hand with lemon tarts."

He wanted to say something more, Elizabeth knew. He made a slight grimace at her change of subject but followed her lead. "Yes, I was made to understand that as well. Shall we see if the actuality bears out the advertisement?"

Elizabeth nodded, grateful to him for his discretion but also anxious at his mode of address. She liked the colonel far too well for her own peace of mind. He had a way of setting her at ease with his competent, confident manner that made her long to rest her cheek against the front of his coat and bide there until she felt stronger. But he was not Mr. Darcy, and she could not dictate the longings of her own heart.

The section ended abruptly. Disappointment flooded through me, and I suppressed a groan. When I looked up, Harriet sat in her customary chair beneath the window, knitting needles in hand. She met my gaze.

"Everything all right, dear?"

"Mr. Darcy kissed Elizabeth? At Rosings?"

Harriet chuckled. "Apparently so, although that part was missing when the manuscript was given to me."

"Are there a lot of holes? In the manuscript, I mean?"

"More than I would like."

"Do you think someone else might have them?"

Harriet shrugged. "I've no idea, really. None of the other ladies are in possession of the missing bits, unfortunately."

I nodded. "Do you have regular meetings, the Formidables, where you discuss these things?" I took a sip of tea, lukewarm but still fragrant. I was intrigued by the idea of the Formidables. How many other secrets did they possess?

Harriet smiled but shook her head. "I don't even know who all the others are, to tell the truth. Only Mrs. Parrot does."

I paused. "Look, Harriet, I'm not exactly sure how I got tangled up in all of this—"

"Because you were kind to an old lady, of course."

"Yes, well, in any case, I don't think I'm the best person to help you decide what you should do with the manuscript. If you don't think you're up to it, the job really should fall to Eleanor."

Harriet snorted. "Definitely not."

I returned my teacup and saucer to the tray.

"Would it really be a bad thing to let Eleanor have the manuscript?" I asked. "She is your daughter, after all. And if she wanted to give it to the university—"

Harriet returned her knitting to the bag at her feet. "The truth is, if Eleanor could get her hands on the manuscript, she'd have it sold before you could say 'Bob's your uncle.'"

"Sell it?" My fingers tightened on the pages in my lap.

"It would fetch quite a good price, I imagine. Enough for Eleanor to give up teaching and work on her own writing."

"But if you asked her not to..."

"Children are a tricky business, Claire. No matter how one tries to mold them, they come into the world a certain shape. It's almost impossible to alter certain…aspects, shall we say, of their personalities."

I thought of my sister and our complicated history. I had often wondered whether we weren't destined from birth for our particular brand of sisterhood. "I understand. At least I think I do."

"Eleanor's very practical. I'm sure that must be a good thing." Harriet's eyes grew misty. "Sadly, her practical nature often fails to account for other people's feelings."

"She loves you," I insisted. "Despite your differences."

"Yes, yes, she does. That's what makes it so difficult." Harriet looked up at me, tears in her eyes. "Love complicates things terribly, you know."

I could only sigh and nod in agreement with her statement.

After that, I helped Harriet clear away the tea things. The small kitchen at the back of the cottage boasted a fine view of the rear garden, but little in the way of modern amenities. Harriet swished the cups and teapot in the ancient sink, and I dried them with a dish towel embossed with pictures of Prince Charles and Lady Diana.

"You said Eleanor wants to sell the manuscript?"

"Yes."

To someone like James, I realized. A publisher.

"Would that be such a bad thing?" I asked. "After all"—I

paused, wondering how to say what I needed to say in a delicate way—"you may find that the income would be helpful—"

Harriet wrung out the dishcloth and hung it over the faucet. "To pay for my care, you mean."

I bit my lip. "Yes. Maybe the money could be put into a trust or something. To pay for whatever you need. And what's left could be given to Jane Austen's House Museum." I'd read about the little cottage in Hampshire on the Internet.

"Yes, it could." But I could see the disappointment in Harriet's eyes. That look, more than anything else that had happened, hurt.

"If you want it to stay secret," I said, "then just give it to Mrs. Parrot."

Harriet rested a hand on the kitchen countertop as if to balance herself.

"The problem with owning something so valuable," she said, "is that after a while, you become too caught up in it. You lose your perspective." She looked at me with those piercing blue eyes. "Perhaps it is the right thing to do to let Eleanor have it. Perhaps I've been wrong, all these years, to keep it hidden away. That's why I need you, Claire. To be my conscience for me."

"I don't know what to say."

"But do you know what to do?" She patted my arm. "That's the more difficult bit, isn't it?"

Her question lay between us, something tangible like a rug or a length of sofa cushion.

"No. I don't. I don't know what to do at all." And not just

with regard to Harriet and her manuscript. I didn't know what to do about James. I didn't know what to do about Neil. I didn't know what to do about Missy. And I certainly didn't know what to do about me.

"Ah, then, perhaps it might help to read some more of the manuscript."

"There's more? I thought you said you didn't know where the missing bits were."

"I'm sure I can turn up something else by tomorrow."

Tomorrow. The word seemed somehow comforting, as if knowing that Harriet would be waiting for me made my troubles a little easier to deal with.

"Tomorrow, then," I said as I hung the dish towel on a little hook beside the sink. I would have wanted to come back to see her in any case, manuscript notwithstanding. "About this time?"

"That would be lovely." Harriet ushered me from the kitchen, and I went with a surprising amount of reluctance to the front door.

"Thank you again for the tea," I said as I left the house. Harriet stood framed in the blue doorway, her smile as soft as the afternoon breeze.

"It was my pleasure," she said, and then the door closed and I was left standing on the path that led from the door to the garden gate.

I turned and let myself out of the gate onto the sidewalk beyond, and then I paused. Back to Christ Church? Or away from it and the problems that awaited me there?

Yet one more decision that I felt ill-equipped to deal with. Denial, though, was often an excellent short-term strategy, so I turned my back toward Christ Church and set off in the opposite direction.

❧❧❧❧❧❧

I hadn't gone far before I realized that someone was following me. I turned and saw an older woman with bright orange hair and a wildly flowered dress marching along a few yards behind me.

I knew without a doubt who it was. I waited as she approached me and then came to a stop a few feet away.

"Mrs. Parrot." I nodded. "I assume you want to speak to me?"

The older woman drew herself up to her full height, which was considerable.

"Yes, Miss Prescott, I did want a word." She peered at me with disapproval. "I'm afraid my friend Harriet isn't thinking very clearly. I want to make sure she doesn't make a mistake. An enormous mistake."

"As big a mistake as sneaking into Christ Church to leave me a note? Or as big a mistake as trashing my room, looking for the manuscript?" The best way to deal with a bully, I'd always been told, was to go on the offensive.

Mrs. Parrot's eyebrows arched. "I hardly a think a note is a mistake. As to the other," she said with a huff. "I never—"

"I'm sure we both want the same thing." I steeled myself to go toe-to-toe with this woman. Yes, she was intimidating, but I was no pushover either. "We want what's best for Harriet."

"Of course." She sniffed. "But the manuscript—"

"Belongs to Harriet." I hitched my purse strap higher on my shoulder. "And it is her right to decide what will happen to it."

Mrs. Parrot took a step toward me. "She agreed, when she joined the Formidables, to keep the existence of *First Impressions* a secret."

"And now she may want to unagree," I shot back.

"She's easily influenced now." Was that real concern in Mrs. Parrot's eyes? "Please, Miss Prescott, help her to do the right thing."

"You can be sure that I will."

We stood there toe-to-toe for a long moment, our gazes locked. Finally she stepped back.

"Very well. As long as you understand what is at stake here."

I nodded. "I'm quite aware what's at stake. An elderly woman's peace and comfort."

Mrs. Parrot pursed her lips. "Quite so."

She spun on one heel and marched away, and I let out a sigh of relief.

There was definitely a reason they called themselves the Formidables, and I was very glad to see the back of Mrs. Parrot. With a little luck, maybe I could avoid the front of her in the future as well.

n Thursday morning, I once again avoided the Hall at breakfast time and paid a return visit to my accommodating Starbucks barista. Much more of this, and I would make prowling Oxford early a habit. I was leaving Starbucks, mocha in hand, when I saw James leaning against a bus stop ten feet away. He was obviously waiting for me.

"Good morning." I tried to remember to breathe and to close my mouth rather than letting my jaw sag at the stubble that framed his square jaw. He didn't look as if he'd slept at all, which, irritatingly enough, made him look all the more attractive. "What are you doing here?"

He pushed away from the bus shelter and stepped toward me. "I followed you."

"That's a little spooky." Only that wasn't the right word for it, really. *Thrilling* would have been more appropriate. I couldn't look at him without remembering that kiss and its devastating effect on me. As well as the devastating effect of his rejection immediately afterward.

He put his hands in his pockets and rocked back and forth on the balls of his feet. "I wanted to apologize, but I couldn't find you after class yesterday. Where were you?"

I twisted the cup of coffee in my hands and tried to play it cool. "I did some sightseeing. Just knocked around Oxford for a bit."

In truth, after my encounter with Mrs. Parrot, I had walked several miles, not really sure of my destination and not paying that much attention to my surroundings. I had stayed close to the river so that I could find my way back. As much as I had walked, I hadn't been able to escape my problems. Still, my solitary ramble had given me a great deal of time to think.

"You were avoiding me, weren't you?" He took a step closer. He was wearing a button-down shirt, the cuffs rolled back to reveal an expensive gold wristwatch.

"No, no. Of course not." Heat flooded my face, and some self-destructive impulse drove the next words out of my mouth. "Actually, yes, I was. Avoiding you, I mean."

I stepped around him and walked down the pavement. It was all I could do not to break out into a jog. Or preferably a sprint. I couldn't have outrun him, though, and in any case he caught up to me within thirty feet.

"Claire, wait. Please."

I stopped, and he swung around in front of me again. "Look, I need to explain some things."

His dark eyes were clouded with some strong emotion. That sight kept me frozen to the spot for a long moment. "Like what kind of things?" I took a drink of my mocha to cover the fact that my hand was shaking.

"About the other night—"

"It's not a big deal. Just a little summer romance."

I hated to even use the R word, but maybe my assertion would clear the air, the decks, my brain. If he was like most men, he would run in the other direction at the mention of romance, and I would realize how futile any hopes I'd had of him had been.

He shook his head. "It's more than a summer fling. You know it is."

"I think you made your feelings pretty clear the other night." I wasn't the kind of woman who had a lot of experience with the opposite sex, especially not with men who were "players."

He took my free hand in his, and once again I thought I might melt at his touch. It really wasn't fair, this immediate and devastating effect he could perpetrate simply by holding my hand.

"Claire, I admit that I panicked. I'm not used to meeting women like you."

I couldn't even bring myself to ask what he meant by that,

because I was pretty sure I knew. Women who weren't sophisticated. Women who didn't know the difference between flirtation and relationship. Women who wore their hearts pinned firmly to their sleeves.

"Like I said, it's not a big deal. And it definitely wasn't worth getting up early just so you could stalk me at Starbucks."

His fingers squeezed mine. "I disagree." He turned then, in the direction of Christ Church, but he kept my hand in his as he started walking. I had to start walking too, or risk being towed along behind him like a barge on the Thames. Thank goodness my mocha had a lid on it.

"James—"

"Just keep moving and listen," he said.

I would like to say that I resisted. That I told him where to get off, in polite terms of course, and then returned to Christ Church on my own. But I was walking hand in hand through the streets of Oxford with a man who was probably the closest living thing to Mr. Darcy I would ever find. Resistance was futile.

"All right. Fine, then." I tried to sound annoyed instead of thrilled.

"You were right," he said, still striding along so that I had to walk faster than normal to keep up with him. "I behaved like a jerk the other night. But you caught me off guard."

"I caught *you* off guard?" I wasn't the one who had swooped in for a little unexpected lip lock.

He scratched the back of his head with his free hand, the

international symbol for male confusion. "When I met you... What I mean is, I didn't expect..."

For a well-educated man, he wasn't displaying spectacular verbal skills. Then again, he was a man. And truth be told, I wasn't attracted to him because of his verbal skills, whatever they might actually be.

"It's okay, James. Really. You kissed me, you regretted it, I should regret it—"

"Should regret it?" He stopped again and spun me to face him.

I almost tripped and fell sideways, but he caught me by my upper arms. Hot liquid sloshed out of the little hole in the lid of my mocha and washed across the back of my hand.

"Ouch." Surprise, more than pain, goosed me, and I dropped the cup. It hit the pavement between us and exploded, brown arcs spraying both of us.

James jumped back and I did too, but not before I was liberally coated with coffee from the waist down. Fortunately, my pants kept me from getting burned. I looked over at James, who was wiping away mocha from the knees of his jeans.

"I'm so sorry," I said and bent toward him to add my efforts to his own.

As I swiped at his legs, I heard a funny kind of rumbling sound. It took me a moment to realize that it was coming from him. I looked up, and he was wearing an expression I'd never seen before. Amusement. Pure unadulterated amusement.

"I'm okay," he said, catching my wrist and pulling me upright.

The coffee hadn't really burned me, but I thought his fingers might. I wondered if it was possible to brand another person with a mere touch. It certainly felt like it.

"I'd say I'm not usually such a klutz," I said with a sigh, "but I'd be lying."

He released my wrist but twisted his hand so that his palm was somehow flat against mine. And then his fingers curled downward and he had me in his grip.

"Claire—"

He was looking at me with those intense dark eyes again, and the ferocity of his gaze would have kept me standing there, stock still, if twelve baristas had come up and doused me with mochas.

"Yes?"

I realized at that moment that we were standing just outside Tom Tower and the Porters' Lodge. I'd hardly noticed how much ground we'd covered on our way back to Christ Church. I glanced around and hoped that none of the other seminar participants were out and about this early to see our strange display of affection. Or at least I thought it was affection.

"I need to tell you something." James's other hand came up to cover where our fingers were joined.

My stomach sank. In the heat of the moment—literally—I'd forgotten that I had some of my own explaining to do, but his words were like a bucket of cold water, reminding me that whatever I might feel for this man, it was based on at least one giant whopper of a lie.

"I've got something to tell you too."

He frowned. "Do you want to go first or should I?"

I knew the answer to that question in my heart, even if I didn't want to admit that I did. Because I knew that I should tell him the truth on the spot, right then and there. But he was looking at me with those gorgeous eyes, and I felt like a movie star or a princess or...

A complete and total fraud.

Because that's what I was, really. None of it was real. Not when it came to James.

Apparently my mocha had contained at least one large lump, and it was now lodged in my throat. I drew a deep breath, thinking I would expel it by simply blurting out the truth. "James, I'm not—"

"Claire?" Another man's voice pierced my consciousness. It came from over my right shoulder. I turned to see who it was, because the voice was familiar. It was a voice from back home. It was—

"Neil? What are you doing here?"

He stood framed in the arch of the gate, half in the shadows of the Porters' Lodge. The weight of James's presence next to me pressed the air from my lungs. I wasn't doing anything wrong, of course. Well, not at the moment. But had Neil seen us walking down the street toward Christ Church, talking so intently? My hand clasped in James's?

"Not exactly the welcome I was hoping for." Neil stepped toward us and eyed James with a narrowed gaze that reminded me of a gunslinger from an old Western movie. His mouth formed a thin line instead of its usual easygoing smile.

"Hello." Stepping forward, he extended his hand. "I'm Neil. Claire's boyfriend."

The blush that rose to my cheeks would have set the entire Midwestern prairie on fire.

James dropped my hand, stiffened, and cast me a disbelieving look. "Boyfriend?"

Neil's gaze flew to me. That clucking noise rattling around in my head was clearly my chickens coming home to roost.

In times of crisis, I had always relied on good manners to get me through. Greeting relatives and friends at the funeral home all those years ago. Meeting with the social workers who regularly checked up on me to make sure I was taking care of Missy. Keeping an entire practice of doctors, nurses, and support staff happy and far from each other's throats. Good manners had always been my lifeline, and I reached for it now.

"Neil," I said, my voice wavering but clear, "this is James. James Beaufort. He's one of the seminar participants." The casual note in my voice practically scorched my tongue. "James, this is, um, Neil. As he said, he's my boyfriend."

I wanted to expire on the spot, and I only regretted there wasn't a convenient manhole right outside Tom Tower that I could disappear down. But this situation…no, this *disaster* was of my own making. For years I'd preached to Missy that she had to clean up her own messes. Not that I'd actually made her clean them up, of course. I would simply scold her and then do it myself. But I'd preached that message long and loud, and now it was clear that the person I should have been preaching to was myself.

James took Neil's outstretched hand as if it were poison. "Welcome to Oxford."

Neil cast him a hard look. "If you don't mind, I'd like to speak to Claire. If I'm not interrupting anything important."

I looked from one man to the other, completely at a loss for words. What was Neil doing here? And when had he developed Neanderthal-like qualities? I'd never seen him more than slightly annoyed, and now I could almost see steam shooting from his ears.

"We were just getting some coffee before our seminar begins," James said. Neil's gaze fell to the overturned cup at our feet. "Unfortunately, Claire had a bit of an accident." To my surprise, James slid a hand around my elbow and cupped it as if he were personally taking charge of my safety.

Neil actually bristled and took another step toward us. He was taller than James. I'd forgotten how tall he was. And where James was the sleek urban type, Neil was more homegrown and all-American.

"I'll take it from here," Neil said, his eyes locked on James.

I would be lying if I didn't say that a little thrill shot through me as I stood there, the two of them looking at each other like boxers sizing up an opponent. Fortunately at that moment, reality burst over me. The only reason the two of them were glowering at each other was because of the lies I had told. That reminder doused any flame of feminine vanity that their male posturing had lit.

James looked from Neil to me. "Claire?" The question encompassed a lot more than just my name. His hand still cupped my elbow, but I could see the confusion in his eyes. "Is it true? Are you involved with him?"

The night my parents were killed, when the police came to the door, I had experienced the same feeling of unreality— although this situation was a tragedy only in the romantic sense, and it was of my own making. But at that moment, I felt that same strange phenomenon I'd experienced all those years before, when time seemed to stand still and I felt as though I were standing outside of myself, watching what was happening to me.

"Yes." I felt the blood drain from my face, and his hand released its grip on my elbow. "Yes, it's true. Neil's my boyfriend."

James's expression, never very open even under the best of circumstances, closed like blinds pulled against the glare of the sun. I felt rather than saw Neil's shoulders drop into a more relaxed posture. As for me, I felt as if I might vomit. Thank goodness I hadn't made any serious inroads on that mocha before I'd dropped it.

"Excuse me." James stepped back and then pivoted on one heel before striding away toward the Porters' Lodge. He moved so quickly, there was no chance of stopping him, of trying to explain. I watched him disappear through Tom Gate, and tears of frustration stung my eyes.

"Claire, what's going on?"

Neil's soft question might as well have been shouted at the top of his lungs, because it had the same effect. I turned to look at him, so familiar, so *normal*, and yet so very out of place in this setting.

Or maybe I was the one who was out of place.

"I can explain," I said, knowing even as I said the words that I really couldn't. How could I ever make Neil understand why I'd tried to be someone I wasn't, when I didn't even really understand it myself?

"Were you with that guy?" Neil's eyes were wide with disbelief. He ran a hand through his hair, and the short-cropped brown strands stood on end. And then the question I'd been dreading the most. "Didn't you tell him about us?"

"Neil—"

But he held up a hand to stop me. "Never mind. I don't think I want to know."

Before I could say anything else, he, too, turned on one heel and walked away with long, swift strides.

"Neil!" I started following him, but after twenty feet and calling his name repeatedly, I realized he wasn't going to stop. I was left standing on the pavement outside Tom Gate, watching him growing smaller and smaller as he headed toward the center of town. Above my head, the bell in the tower began to chime the hour. And in my heart, it felt like a death knell.

 had no idea where to look for Neil, but I did know where to find James. The bell chiming in Tom Tower should have reminded me, if nothing else. Eleanor would be calling the seminar to order, and it was James's day to present his paper. I would rather have faced a firing squad, but since that wasn't an option, I set off instead across the quad toward Eleanor Gibbons's lair, my pants covered with coffee and my mind in turmoil.

This time, I was the last one to take my seat. The rest of the group chatted quietly, and James sat next to Eleanor, talking with her in low, urgent tones. He glanced up when I entered the room, but his expression never changed, and he didn't acknowledge my presence.

I sat down between Martin and Olga and tried not to cry.

"Good morning again, everyone." Eleanor called the group to order with her usual brisk efficiency. "Let's begin right away, shall we?" She turned to James. "I'm sure you've some intriguing new point of view on our novel for us to consider."

"Possibly." He opened a monogrammed leather portfolio and looked around the room without actually looking at me. "I'm a businessman, not an academic, so take that into consideration."

Martin chuckled in sympathy, Rosie and Louise made their usual soothing noises, and the cardiologist simply looked bored. Olga looked entranced, but maybe she was just enjoying looking at James.

"And what's your paper entitled?" Eleanor asked.

The corners of his mouth tightened. "Love and Deception: What's the Difference?"

I could see the words in my mind as they must have been typed on the page he held in his hand, and I cringed.

"Do begin," Eleanor said encouragingly. She shot me a look that I couldn't quite decipher, but I thought she might have had a gleam of triumph in her eye.

I wouldn't have been surprised if she knew about James and me spending so much time together. I also wouldn't have been surprised to know she'd drawn her own conclusions from that information and the fact that James was clearly ignoring me.

"In *Pride and Prejudice*," James was saying, "Austen manipulates her characters for the purposes of her own satisfaction, not to portray the truth about love."

There were a few low, questioning murmurs, and I tried to

look politely interested but not overly involved. Certainly not as if I was hanging on every word that came out of his mouth.

"Elizabeth Bennet justifies her change in feelings for Mr. Darcy because he saves her sister Lydia. Certainly she would have been grateful, but if he had been poor or unattractive, she would not have imagined herself in love with him." James's voice burned like fire now. At least it seemed that way to me. The members of the group were nodding, some intently and others looking as if they were in danger of nodding off. "Austen constructs a scenario where Elizabeth can justify her selfish choice of Darcy with the illusion of love."

Illusion? Who in the history of English literature had ever read any of Austen's novels and come to the conclusion that she'd really been engaged in a monumental fakeout of her readers? Well, given what little I knew about true academic scholarship, someone probably had. The important question was, why had James come to that conclusion even before the scene outside the Porters' Lodge?

Embarrassment still stained my cheeks, and I was distinctly uncomfortable whenever his gaze happened to move over me. But as he continued to expound on his theory, I realized something. He had to have written this paper long before he even met me, whatever he might have told me earlier. No, these sentiments were not the result of my duplicity or Neil's unexpected arrival. James had taken issue with Austen's version of love long before I ever entered the picture.

I glanced around the circle and caught Eleanor's eye. She was looking at me with both contempt and pleasure. I quickly shifted my gaze elsewhere, but no matter where I focused, I couldn't escape my own thoughts. Or my own guilt. Somewhere beyond the walls of Christ Church, Neil was wandering the same streets that I had wandered, trying to figure out why he'd ever asked me out in the first place. And right in this very room, I was trying to figure out the same thing.

Who had I become in the past few days? Or was the question more serious than that? Perhaps the real puzzle was, who had I become in the years since my parents' death?

For the second time that morning, I felt as if I might vomit. I lurched to my feet, stumbling over Martin's sensible professor-type shoes, and headed toward the door.

"I'm sorry. Excuse me." By the time I made it outside the circle, I was seeing stars. I could only pray that I wouldn't trip on the stairs or otherwise land in a heap before I could escape.

✦✦✦✦✦

Almost on instinct, I made my way to the river. I collapsed on the grass and took in deep gulps of air. At midmorning, the path along the bank was largely deserted, and only the occasional punt glided past. I'd observed the flat-bottom boats on the little stretch of river and decided they looked deceptively innocent, like Missy just before she asked me for a gigantic favor. Even the laughing young college students seemed to find them hard to maneuver, the unwieldy length of the pole often slipping from their hands and leaving them stranded midstream. I had witnessed one young man take a headfirst tumble into the river while attempting to impress his girlfriend.

I sighed and closed my eyes in an effort to find some measure of calm.

"Ahoy, landlubber."

My eyes popped open at the sound of that deep, familiar voice.

The last sight I'd ever expected to see was Neil standing on the back of a punt, poling the little boat along. He drew the punt up to the bank and brought it to a stop a few feet from where I sat on the grass.

"Hey." I didn't know what to say.

"Can I give you a lift?" His enigmatic expression gave me no clue as to what he was thinking.

"I'm not sure why you'd want to." I still felt the sting of shame that had struck me earlier that morning. That continued, even now, to burn.

He looked serious, his jaw tense, but at least he'd stopped when he saw me.

"We need to talk, Claire."

I nodded, but it took all the courage I could muster not to turn and run back toward Christ Church.

"I'm supposed to be at Harriet's soon." Which was true, but it was a while before she'd be expecting me.

"I have no idea who Harriet is," Neil said with a frown. "I'm thinking of abandoning ship whenever I find a pub." He reached out a hand. "You're welcome to come along."

What was I supposed to say? What could I say?

"All right."

The fact that Neil would want me within ten feet of him after what had happened with James amazed me. And frightened me a little too. He wasn't the vengeful type—not in the least. But I wouldn't have blamed him if he'd succumbed to the temptation to tip the punt over—and me into the river.

"Watch your step." He held out his free hand while the other gripped the pole that held the boat steady.

I scrambled to my feet and slung my purse over my shoulder. Then I reached out and took his hand.

A bolt of pure sensation shot up my arm and stunned me.

"Claire? It's okay. I've got you." His gaze locked with mine, holding me as firmly as his hand held mine.

I forced myself to breathe. To move my feet and step into the boat. To release his hand as I sank onto one of the wooden planks that served as seats.

Neil? I'd felt a zing with Neil? In the eighteen months I'd known him, that had never happened before. A pleasant warmth, maybe. A sense of comfort and connection. But not this kind of energy or awareness. There had never been a zing.

"I'm fine," I said, more to reassure myself than him.

"Good. All right, then. Let's see if I can get this thing moving."

I looked up at him. His hair, backlit by the sun, was edged with gold, and his face was in shadow. His forearms flexed each time he pulled the pole up and then dropped it down again to push us farther down the river. I was mesmerized by them.

"Why are you even speaking to me?" I managed to ask when I finally tore my eyes away from his arms.

He hesitated in his movements for the briefest fraction of a second. If I hadn't been watching him so intently, I would have missed it. I'd always found Neil to be an open book, but I knew at that moment that I'd been wrong to assume there wasn't more to him than what he revealed to the world. Was it that I had missed the obvious signs, or was it that I hadn't wanted to know more about what went on in his head? Shame washed over me, because I knew the answer to that question, and it wasn't a flattering one. I hadn't consciously been keeping him at arm's length, but the effect was the same.

"Claire?" He pulled the pole out of the water, but instead of dropping it again, he turned it horizontally and laid it along the length of the boat. Then he lowered himself to the plank opposite mine. The punt drifted toward the bank, grazed it, and then came to a stop. "We have to talk about what happened this morning." He looked at me, and I could see the hurt in his eyes. Guilt poured over me. "Do you want to start or should I?" he asked.

I had known that the moment of reckoning would come, but that didn't make me dread it any less.

"I'm sorry." I didn't know what else to say. Well, I did, but I didn't want to say it. I wasn't used to looking like a villainess. I'd always imagined myself a heroine, like Elizabeth Bennet.

"I understand you're sorry. What I don't understand is why you let it happen."

I looked up into his eyes and saw that he genuinely meant what he said. "Why are you being so calm about this?" I asked.

He reached out and took my hand, and there was that zing again. I wanted to snatch my hand back. I didn't deserve his tenderness, but I needed it more than I was ashamed to receive it.

He cleared his throat. "You may want to wait to decide how calm I am. Right now I'm just trying to figure out what's going on."

I left my hand in his and stared at the bottom of the punt. "I don't really know how it happened. One moment I was sitting there, in the Junior Common Room, looking over the list of attendees. And the next thing I knew, James showed up and..."

I couldn't believe I was telling him the truth. If ever I was going to lie, now would have been the time. But I couldn't. Not while Neil was looking at me that way.

"He's a good-looking guy, I guess." Neil's tone was gruff. "I know I haven't paid you as much attention as I should have. Maybe you just needed—"

"It's not just because you took me for granted." I shocked myself as much as Neil with those words. "Maybe I was feeling ignored. I don't know. I guess I swallowed my resentment. But that's not the reason I developed...feelings for James."

"Then why?"

I hung my head and studied the bottom of the punt. "I don't know."

He paused, and I saw the shadow of pain in his eyes. "I just wish you'd been honest with me. That would have been a lot easier." He gave a crooked smile. "It would have saved me a lot of money on a plane ticket too."

"Why are you here?" I hadn't really had a chance to ask, since everything had happened so quickly. "You never said anything about coming over. In fact, I wasn't even sure you were paying attention when I said I was leaving."

He scowled now for the first time since I'd gotten in the punt. "After you left, I realized—" He broke off and cleared his throat. "I realized that maybe I haven't put as much time into our relationship as I should have."

"Neil, I'm so sorry."

He let go of my hand and rested his forearms on his knees. They were well-muscled from his regular workouts and his weekly pickup basketball game. I'd always taken his strength for granted. He was terrific around the house. He'd replaced the facings on my kitchen cupboards, helped me to retile my bathroom, changed my flat tire when I'd gotten stuck in the rain. But now I looked at his arms and realized that where I really wanted them to be was around me.

The thought shocked me. Neil and I had a comfortable, easy relationship. Maybe too easy. And suddenly I was feeling zings and having carnal thoughts about his forearms.

Confusion and shame are a potent cocktail and never do much for a woman's good sense.

"I guess it happened because...well, because I suspected that you don't really need me," I blurted out.

He jerked back as if I'd slapped him.

"Need you? No, I don't," he said, anger streaming into his voice for the first time. "Not to take care of me. Not like Missy needs you just to get through the day. To function." He paused. "But I want you, Claire. I want to be with you. Build a life with you. I want that very much."

He shook his head. "I'm not the only one who got taken for granted in this relationship. You can only think about what you *should* do. For your sister. For your job. Not about what you really *want* to do." He took my hand again. "And that's the question, isn't it? What do *you* want, Claire? Do you want this James guy on the strength of a few days of flirtation? Do you want me? Or do you just want to go on hiding behind your sister, pretending that you have no needs of your own? Because someday you'll wake up and Missy's kids will be grown. Maybe Missy will be too." He gave a bitter laugh. "Someday she might not need you anymore, not like she does now. And you'll be alone."

"That's not fair." My response was automatic. His words hurt, but only because they had the sting of truth. "Since when is it a crime to be responsible for people you love?"

He reached up and ran a hand through his hair as he had done earlier that morning, and once again the strands stood on end. "It's not a crime, Claire, to want the best for the people you love. But it's not an escape hatch either."

"What do you think I'm escaping from?" I flung the question at him out of my own hurt, but it didn't make his observations any less true or any less painful.

He shrugged. "I wish I knew. Maybe I could help you get away from whatever it is if I did."

The sorrow in his voice was my undoing. "Could we just keep going, please?" I said. "I'm going to be late." I reached for the pole and nudged him with it. "Maybe we can finish the psychoanalysis later."

I couldn't look at him after I said that. Instead I focused on the thick, green surface of the river. After a long moment, Neil stood up and, taking up his position at the back of the boat, slid the pole once again into the water.

"Just tell me when we get where you need to be," he said in a flat, emotionless voice. "Because I have no idea where that is."

All I could do was nod and try to keep from falling apart before I could get away. By the time we reached the next landing where he could put me ashore, the silence had grown into a living entity. I scrambled from the punt, relieved to have firm ground beneath my feet again.

"What are you going to do?" I asked him.

He frowned and leaned against the pole. "I don't know. A lot of thinking, I guess." He lifted the pole and used it to push away from the bank again. "I'll find you later."

"Okay." What else could I do but agree? "I'll be back at Christ Church in a couple of hours."

He nodded. "I'll look for you."

We both hesitated, gazes locked, each of us desperately trying to understand the other. After a long moment, he sighed and turned his attention to the punt.

"Good-bye." With one strong push, he sent the little boat back into the current.

"Good-bye."

I stood there on the bank and watched him drift into the distance for the second time in one day.

Neil was right. I had taken him for granted, just as he had me. The vein of weakness in our relationship had been exposed, and I knew, as well as anyone, that a weak spot was always where you would expect something to break. I just hadn't expected that weak spot with Neil to feel as if it were smack-dab in the middle of my heart.

arriet was in her front garden when I approached the cottage. She sat on a little stool near a lush bank of flowers, twisting off random bits and then reaching lower to pluck a weed or two from the ground below. She looked like a mother hen tending her brood of chicks. In fact, as I approached, I thought I heard her clucking to the plants.

"Good morning, Harriet." I spoke softly so that I wouldn't startle her.

She turned to me, her smile bright. "Claire? You're early today."

I stepped through the gate. "I know it's not our usual time—"

"Never too early to greet a friend, dear." She plucked one final dead flower from a large bush and levered herself up off the stool.

I stepped forward and reached out a hand to help her, but she waved me away.

"No, no. I can manage." The stool was a collapsible, three-legged affair. She shut it and laid it across the wheelbarrow that stood next to her. "Now, then, tell me everything. What's brought you here?" She gave me a long, measuring look. "Shouldn't you be in Eleanor's seminar?"

"Yes. But something's happened."

"Well, yes, of course. Otherwise you wouldn't be here. Would a cup of tea help?"

I was learning, even in my brief time in England, that a cup of tea almost always helped. I didn't know whether it was the caffeine, the warmth, or the simple fact of having someone else do something kind, but a soothing cup of tea in Harriet Dalrymple's cottage was fast becoming my lifeline to sanity.

"Yes, it would help. Thank you." Although I realized, at that moment, that simply being in Harriet's presence helped more than anything. It had been many years since anyone had mothered me. And though Harriet may have been a relative stranger and not entirely clear in her mind, she was the closest thing to a mother that I had experienced in a very long time.

"Well, come along then." She nodded to the wheelbarrow. "If you don't mind putting that in the shed over there"—she waved in the general direction of the side of the cottage—"I'll put the kettle on."

"Okay. Sure." I reached over and grabbed the handles of the wheelbarrow and started off in the direction she had indicated.

"Oh, and I've good news," Harriet called over her shoulder as she moved toward the cottage's blue front door.

"What's that?" I twisted around to look at her.

"I found more of the manuscript," she said, smiling. "Never thought to look in the garden shed until this morning, but there it was."

I looked down at the wheelbarrow in front of me and couldn't help but grin.

Of course. A little Jane Austen mixed among the trowels and spades and potting soil. Where else would Harriet have kept it?

❧❧❧❧❧❧

"I don't know if these bits go together," Harriet said when she handed me the pages this time. "They seem to be different sections." She smiled. "They are two of the best bits, though."

I'd thought what I'd already read were pretty good bits myself, so I reached for the pages eagerly. Armed with the manuscript and a cup of tea on the table in front of me, I put aside the turmoil of the day and focused on the elegant, if old-fashioned, handwriting on the page.

First Impressions
Chapter Seventeen

Elizabeth was walking about the park the next morning, delighted to have half an hour to herself, when she passed a large yew tree and followed an abrupt turn in the path, only to find Mr. Darcy striding toward her. He had two large dogs with him for company and a ferocious scowl upon his face.

"Miss Bennet." He stopped and motioned for the dogs to come to heel. "Good morning to you." Since the night of that infamous kiss, he had avoided her assiduously.

"Mr. Darcy." Her heart beat furiously beneath her pelisse, and she wished she'd not removed her bonnet. It dangled down her back, secured only by the ribbons still tied and now pressing against her throat.

Silence fell between them until he cleared his throat and spoke once more. "Miss de Bourgh is in good health today, I trust?"

"Yes. She is with her mother. My presence was not required." She kept her tone civil, even though her thoughts were not. "Is there anything I may do for you, sir, since I am at my leisure?"

Heat rose to Elizabeth's cheeks when she realized that he might interpret her remark in quite a different manner than she had intended it. "I did not mean—" She could not prevent the flush that rose to her cheek.

"Your countenance reveals far more than you would wish," he said in matter-of-fact tones, "although I find that it is your eyes, for the most part, which give voice to your thoughts."

"My eyes?" Elizabeth knew she sounded like the veriest slowtop, but she stumbled to find the right words. Or any words, for that matter.

"They are quite expressive." He moved closer, as did the dogs, and Elizabeth suppressed the urge to spin upon her heel and flee.

"I'm sure I don't mean to express... That is, I mean to say, I have no knowledge of—" She broke off and could only look at him weakly.

Unexpectedly, Mr. Darcy lifted his arm and offered it to her. "Walk with me, Miss Bennet. It appears we have a great deal to discuss."

"Very well." She laid tentative fingers upon his sleeve and turned to walk with him from the way she'd come.

"You have used your charms and inducements to great effect," he said as they strolled at a leisurely pace. The dogs stayed obediently to heel, and Elizabeth wondered whether everyone in Mr. Darcy's life did the same. "Great effect, indeed."

"I'm sorry?" Surely she had not heard him correctly. "I have no idea what you mean."

Mr. Darcy turned his head to look at her, although the height of his shirt points and the restrictive knot of his cravat made it rather a difficult exercise.

"It was your design, was it not, to entice me into this folly? Fitzwilliam claims you are innocent of such a scheme, but I do not agree."

Fitzwilliam? She collected that he meant the colonel. "I know of no scheme, sir, of which I am a part."

Fanciful wishes, perhaps. Even the imprudence

of allowing herself to think at all of someone such as Mr. Darcy of Pemberley. But a scheme?

"Do you deny that you have set your cap for me?"

If Elizabeth had possessed any remnants of pride, his words surely destroyed them. Her hand tightened on his arm. He looked down at the point where her fingers rested upon his coat sleeve.

"I have done no such thing, sir."

"Do you mean to say you have succeeded in snaring me without conscious effort?"

"Snared you, sir?"

"Only the poor marry for love, Miss Bennet." His eyes were fixed on Rosings. "My considerations are quite different."

"Yes, obviously. You are certainly above such human considerations as love."

He turned to look at her, his dark gaze fixed on her face. "You mock me, then, Miss Bennet?"

"No, sir, I do not."

He released a heavy sigh and laid his free hand over her fingers. They were drawing closer to the house. Only a few moments were left before they would reach the terrace.

"You would have me say it plainly, then?" He shook his head. "From the first day we met, you gained my notice. I knew you were beneath me in birth, fortune, and situation. Even had your father lived—"

Elizabeth gasped, and his hand pressed her fingers

more tightly. "You need not speak, Mr. Darcy, of such matters." She pulled her hand away. "In fact, I insist that you do not."

By this time, they had indeed reached the steps to the terrace. He drew her to a stop. She looked up at him to find an unexpected emotion in his eyes. If she hadn't been acquainted with Mr. Darcy's character, she might have labeled it as fear. As it was, she thought it might be strong apprehension.

"I am in no position to offer you marriage, Miss Bennet."

A door opened at the other end of the terrace, and she heard footsteps. Someone was coming.

"I cannot ask for your hand. My duty to my family... Well, you are well enough acquainted with my aunt to know what is expected of me."

"What reply am I to make to such a statement?" Elizabeth felt the first stirrings of anger. "You tell me that you have condescended enough to care for me, though I am vastly inferior in every way. You hint of strong affection. Of love. Yet you are ashamed of your feelings."

"Is it not natural that I should be?"

Pain filled his gaze, and for a moment Elizabeth felt pity for him. He loved her. The realization tightened her chest and made her wish for a strong arm to support her. But his was the only arm close enough to lean on, and she could not ask for it.

"I have never sought your good opinion, sir. And if you

have loved me against your will, against your judgment, even against your character, then you must look to your own heart for the source of such treachery. It was not I that led you down the garden path."

"Elizabeth." He reached for her hand once more. "If I could, I would allow my actions to follow my heart. If I were to ask ... If I were free to ask ..." He shook his head. "But I am not."

Elizabeth drew herself up to her full height. "You are free, sir. As free as any man in England. And my answer would be——"

"Wait! Where's the last page?" I looked up at Harriet in panic and then back at the single sheet of paper in my lap. I flipped it over, hoping that the rest of the sentence might have been written on the back, but it was blank.

"Oh dear, did I misplace the ending?" Harriet rose from her chair beneath the window and looked around the sitting room as if she'd never seen it before. "There might be a few more bits about somewhere. Let me think."

I wanted to leap up from the sofa and start to rifle through the room myself, but I didn't want to scare Harriet. Here I had reached the climactic moment in the novel, only to find that I had no way to discover Elizabeth's answer. And I needed to know her answer. The crumbling manuscript pages that had started out for me as a mere curiosity had become vital—perhaps the key to my own convoluted situation.

"Please, Harriet. Are you sure you don't have the last page

here somewhere? Maybe it's still in the garden shed." I sprang up from the sofa. "I'll go and check."

"I suppose it might. Yes, have a look in the shed. I'll see what I can find here."

I didn't waste any time on a reply but instead raced out of the room and out the blue door. In moments I was standing in the middle of the small shed at the bottom of Harriet's garden.

I quickly scanned the shelves and stacks of odds and ends. A large window allowed me enough light to search, but ten minutes spent moving various implements and bits of detritus from one place to another yielded no results. I should have asked Harriet where in the shed she had found the last section of the manuscript. I had almost given up when I spied the corner of a yellowed piece of paper protruding from beneath a watering can. I squealed and reached for it, whisking away the watering pot lest it should drip upon the precious page. I held the paper carefully to the light.

"Yes!" I jumped in the air with delight. "There's more." I bent my head to make out the words.

Elizabeth knew she should have returned to Brighton to supervise Lydia's flirtations with the parade of redcoats who took tea in Mrs. Bennet's lodgings, but the inducement of a London respite with her beloved aunt and uncle Gardiner proved far too strong. She would have to rely upon her mother's oversight of Lydia and Kitty. Surely a few weeks would not matter. And she would find it far easier to procure a new situation in town where she might visit the agencies directly, since Lady Catherine had turned her out without a reference.

"Elizabeth!" Jane waited at the door of her aunt and uncle's home in Cheapside when the hackney deposited Elizabeth on the pavement.

The comfort of Jane's arms around her proved her undoing. She allowed the balm of sisterly consolation to pour into her heart even as she cried in her sister's embrace.

I looked up from the manuscript. "Sisterly consolation?" I turned through the yellowed page over as I had done earlier, but there was no further writing. "But what happened?" I asked the empty air around me. "Did she refuse Darcy? What about the colonel? How does it end?"

I needed to know. If I knew how Elizabeth found her happy ending, perhaps I might be able to figure out my own. Perhaps I might know what choice to make in my own life if I could just get a little guidance from a fictional character and from an author who had been dead for almost two hundred years.

arriet insisted before I left that I must come back the next day to see if she could locate the final section of the manuscript. I returned to Christ Church discouraged and confused, and when I got to my room, there was yet another note taped to my door. I expected it to be from Eleanor, fussing at me for leaving the seminar early, or from Mrs. Parrot, demanding the return of the manuscript. But when I got close enough to read it, I saw that the handwriting was far too masculine for either possibility.

Meet me at the Bear, it said, and it was signed simply *N*.

I stood there on the small landing, awash with uncertainty. The truth was that at this point, I didn't know which man I wanted, or whether either man truly wanted me. But Neil and I had unfinished business. Avoiding him wouldn't change that.

I did take long enough to change out of my coffee-splattered clothing and into a light summer dress. A dab of makeup and some bracelets couldn't hurt when it came to the self-esteem department. I emerged from the Meadow Building fifteen minutes and a slightly less bruised ego later.

The Bear was a landmark pub just around the corner from Christ Church. It dated back as far as some of the earliest colleges and was now famous for its collection of neckties hanging from the walls inside. It was early afternoon now, and the crowd spilled out the doors and onto the long wooden tables and benches outside. I approached slowly, looking for Neil among the eclectic collection of students, tourists, and townies.

"Claire." I heard him call my name, but it was a moment before I could pick him out from the crowd. He sat alone at one of the long tables off to the side of the building, a pint glass in front of him. He looked as if he'd been there awhile.

"Hey." I sat down on the bench next to him rather than put the width of the table between us. Whatever we were going to say, I didn't want us to be shouting it for all of Oxford to hear.

"Do you want something to drink?" He nodded toward the door of the pub.

"A Diet Coke?" Maybe the sugar-caffeine combo would help to clear my head. "But I can get it."

"Nope. Stay put." He managed to free his long legs and get to his feet. "I'll be back in a sec."

He disappeared inside the pub, and I sat with my back to

the table, watching the foot traffic on the cobbled street. I recognized a few faces, participants in other seminars at Christ
Church, but I didn't really know anyone. That is, I didn't know
anyone until I saw the dark-haired man lounging against the
building wall opposite me.

James.

He was staring at me, his brooding gaze intent. I tried to
look away, but I couldn't. He realized that I'd seen him and
shifted his stance slightly, crossing his arms in front of him.
Had he been there all along, watching Neil? Or had he happened by, seen me, and stopped to see what was going on?

I didn't really want to have my heart-to-heart with Neil
while James watched us like a hawk, but I couldn't get up and
go over to talk with him either. Not when Neil might reappear
at any moment. So we just stared at each other, and I tried to
figure out what it all meant. If I really loved Neil, would I have
ever been attracted to James in the first place? And if I truly
had fallen for James, wouldn't I be ready to give Neil the old "I
hope we can be friends" speech? But the truth was that I wasn't
ready to do either of those things. No, I was well and truly
stuck between two men whom I probably didn't deserve.

"Here you go." A glass of Diet Coke thunked down on the
table in front of me.

"Oh. Thanks." I quickly averted my gaze and prayed that
Neil hadn't seen James lounging against the wall across the
way.

Neil took his seat beside me. Lines of weariness fanned out
from the corners of his eyes. He was still jet-lagged, I realized

with a jolt. The poor man was no doubt exhausted to begin with, and I certainly hadn't made things any easier.

"Look, I'm sorry this has been such a disaster. It never occurred to me that you would—"

"Turn up and spoil your fun?" For the first time, he sounded truly bitter. He took a long drink from his pint and then grimaced. "Sorry. Sarcasm's not going to help."

"I guess I'm just...stunned that you're here."

"I was going more for happy."

Now it was my turn to grimace. "I know. And I am. Happy, I mean."

He laughed. "Really? Could have fooled me."

I couldn't turn my head to look, but I would have sworn I still felt James's gaze piercing me. This conversation with Neil would have been difficult enough under the best of circumstances. The last thing I needed was the romantic complication of a lifetime watching me while I tried to sort everything out. I swiveled on the bench so that my back was to James, but it meant I had to look at Neil out of the corner of my eye. Not ideal, but perhaps the best I could do at the moment.

"Neil, why did you come, really? Surprises aren't really your cup of tea."

He sat with one hand around his glass and the other on his knee. His jeans, polo shirt, and baseball cap gave him that all-American look I'd always liked, but it was a far cry from James's expensive designer clothing.

Neil shrugged. "I guess I thought it would be romantic. I guess I thought..." He looked past me, his eyes hazy as if he were looking not at anything outside himself but rather at something within.

Finally his eyes turned to mine. "I guess I thought I would bring you this."

He reached in his pocket and pulled out a small blue velvet box. He opened it, and I gasped.

The diamond winked in the sun. It was a plain stone on a platinum band, neither too large nor too small. Not fancy, but respectable. Kind of like Neil himself.

"Oh, Neil."

"Yeah, well, my mistake." He flipped the lid of the box closed and stuffed it back in his pocket.

Tears sprang to my eyes, and I had to look away, but that meant looking at James, which only made things worse. I turned back to the man sitting next to me and saw that Neil had been watching me as closely as I had been watching James. I blushed and took a long drink from my glass of Diet Coke in an effort to appear disinterested, but I wasn't fooling anyone. Not Neil, and certainly not myself.

"Are you in love with him?" Neil jerked his head in James's direction.

This time I looked directly at James. Even at this distance, I could see his strong cheekbones and firm jaw. He was like a Michelangelo statue come to life. But he was also moody, restless, and more than a little arrogant.

"I don't know."

Neil finished the last of the dark amber liquid in his glass.

"I think that's my cue." He rose from the bench, and I did the same.

I reached up as if to stop him. "I'm sorry, Neil."

"I'm not. If I hadn't come over here, I would never have known."

Guilt surged through me. "I never meant to deceive you. It never occurred to me that I could. Not until this week."

Neil's smile was slight but held a hint of humor. "Well, they say travel is broadening."

"Neil—" Tears choked my throat, and I couldn't get the rest of the words out.

"Don't say it." Now he had tears in his eyes too, which made me feel even worse. "If I head for the airport, I might be able to get a flight out tonight."

"You're leaving?"

"What do you want me to do, Claire? Hang around and watch you with Lover Boy over there?"

He had a point, but the idea of losing Neil sent waves of grief washing over me. I'd gotten so used to having him in my life. What would I do without him?

"No," I said. "Of course I wouldn't want that. But you've flown all this way. Don't you want to...I don't know...do some touristy things?"

He reached out and cupped my cheek with his hand. The warmth of his touch almost melted me. "Claire, I didn't come all this way to go sightseeing." He sighed. "I came to be with you."

I closed my eyes and laid my hand against the back of his,

holding it in place against my face. "I never meant for any of this to happen."

"There's intending and there's allowing."

I opened my eyes, startled by the intensity of his voice. "Neil, it just happened."

He shook his head. "It does make me wonder, though."

"Wonder what?"

"Whether all this"—he waved a hand toward James—"is really about him. Or if it's about punishing me."

I grasped his wrist and pulled his hand away from my face. "I can't believe you would say that."

He put his hands on his hips and eyed me as if I were a bug under a microscope. "Maybe it's time to take a long hard look at yourself, Claire. Before you do an emotional body slam on some other poor guy."

And then he turned and walked away. I watched him as he melted into the crowd, frozen in place by his parting words.

They say that the truth hurts. That would certainly have explained the agony that held me paralyzed as Neil's head, the last part of him that I could see, disappeared around the corner. James, too, was gone from his spot by the wall, and I was left, once again, alone.

❧❧❧❧❧

Emotionally and physically exhausted, I made my way back to my room at Christ Church and succumbed to the afternoon heat. I fell into bed and a deep, dreamless sleep. But at the sound of thick raindrops slapping against the window panes, I bolted upright. After so many days of unrelenting heat, the rain burst over the parched Oxford landscape. I needed to be outside in the elements, a part of this sudden release from the heat that had held me captive all week.

I hurried down the stairs and slipped outside the walls of the college. The wide gravel avenue that separated Christ Church from its meadow crunched beneath my feet. The cows that awakened me at an ungodly hour every morning were nowhere to be seen. Instead, the tall brown grass lay flattened by the weight of the rain. I waded into the grass, already soaked to the skin, and let the water fall on my head and my shoulders, and in rivulets down my back.

"What are you doing?"

I whirled around to find James standing a few feet away on the gravel avenue, safely sheltered by a large black umbrella.

"I'm getting soaked. That's what I'm doing."

"Why?" His mouth tightened, but I couldn't tell if it was from amusement or exasperation.

I shrugged. "I have no idea."

But that wasn't the truth. I knew perfectly well why I had sought out the baptism of the rain. I needed a source for the forgiveness I needed, a fresh start, a clean slate. Because on my solitary walk back from the pub to my room, I'd realized that Neil was right.

The rain stopped as suddenly as it started. The ponderous clouds broke apart, as if dispersed by the hand of God. James lowered his umbrella and snapped it closed.

"You feel guilty."

Since that was as obvious as the rain, I didn't reply, just shifted my weight from one foot to the other like the liar I was.

James moved toward me, and even then, after everything that had happened, his nearness made my breath catch in my throat and my knees tremble. "I assume that since Neil left and you're still here, things didn't work out."

I bit my lip, but then released it quickly so that he wouldn't notice. Until I met James, I'd never lied to a man. Now I was lying to two of them. I had lost Neil. That much was clear. And now it was simply a matter of time—and some belated honesty—before I lost James too.

"I have to tell you something." I forced my tongue and lips to utter the clichéd words. They were clichéd for good reason. Like the mournful tolling of bells, they gave the listener fair warning that doom was imminent.

He grimaced. "You should have told me about Neil in the beginning. But I've thought it over, and it doesn't matter." He let the umbrella fall to the ground and took my hands in his. "We can make a fresh start, Claire. Build a new life together."

I started. "Really?" That was the last thing I had expected him to say.

"I know you have your practice to consider."

Now my knees sagged instead of trembled, and I wished we were anywhere that had a bench or a chair, because I wasn't sure my legs would support me for much longer.

"Actually, I don't," I said through chattering teeth.

"Don't what?"

"I don't have a practice to consider."

His face tightened in confusion. "But—"

"James, I'm not a pediatrician. I don't have a medical license. I never even went to college."

"But—"

What was the old expression? *In for a penny, in for a pound?*

"I'm an office manager for a group of pediatricians. Or I was. That part's true, at least." The heat of shame flooded my body, and I stopped shivering.

"You're not a doctor?" He spoke with care, enunciated each syllable with precision.

"No."

"Another lie."

"Yes."

"How many more are there?"

I dropped my gaze, unable to look him in the eye anymore.

"How many, Claire?"

"Just one."

"And that is?"

"The one I've been telling myself. That you're some kind of Mr. Darcy."

"Mr. Darcy?" He laughed. "Claire—"

"I know. It's all my little fantasy that I cooked up because—" I stopped, because even though Neil was right, I wasn't ready to admit it out loud yet. "Well, that doesn't matter. What does matter is that I was with you for all the wrong reasons, and I'm sorry."

His face had gone immobile, as if it were carved from stone.

"I'm sorry, James. I don't know what else to say."

"Claire—"

"I think I'd better go." Maybe it was cowardice, but I'd undertaken all the honesty I could for one day. Dripping wet from head to toe, I sloshed back toward Christ Church and sought the sanctuary of my room. Tomorrow was Friday, the last day of the seminar. I would skip it, of course, and stay out of sight in my room. Or perhaps go see Harriet and tell her good-bye. A shame that I would never know how that first version of *Pride and Prejudice* ended, but maybe it was better not to know. Maybe it was better to bury my Mr. Darcy fantasy once and for all, here on its native soil.

I had definitely learned my lesson, and it had been at a very steep price.

That night I didn't dream about a handsome, arrogant hero who swept me off my feet and saved me from a life of drudgery. No, I dreamed about cabinet facings and bathroom tiles. About patience and flat tires.

I dreamed about two familiar, strong arms that had helped me every bit as much as they had held me. Two arms that I now missed desperately. And the man attached to them who meant far more to me than I had ever allowed myself to admit.

he cows lowing in the meadow outside my window woke me early on Friday morning. Exhausted by the events of the week, I tried to fall back into the oblivion of sleep, but no matter how tired my body might be, my mind was a hive of activity.

Neil was gone, James knew me for the fraud I was, and my seminar leader was my mortal enemy. I had made as big a mess of my life on this side of the Atlantic as I had on the other. I burrowed my head deeper into the pillow and let waves of homesickness wash over me.

I just wanted to go back to Kansas City, back to the life I'd had before I lost my job, the life I'd taken for granted. I would have given anything for a Saturday night on Neil's sofa watching a baseball game, or a Monday morning wiping the disgusting bits of food out of the microwave at work. I'd have been happy even to drive Phillip to the airport at the crack of dawn or babysit for Missy when she needed a night out with her girlfriends.

After tossing and turning for another half hour, I gave up on the idea of sleep. Showered and dressed, I made my way not to the Hall for breakfast but to the sanctuary of the Master's Garden. I took refuge on a wooden bench beneath the shelter of a tree, the magnificent green lawn spread out before me and still wet with morning dew.

I retrieved my cell phone from my purse and then entered Missy's familiar number. More than anything, I needed to hear a friendly voice.

The phone rang once, twice, then several more times. Finally I heard popping and scratching noises and at length a bleary "Hello?"

"Missy? It's me. Claire."

"Claire?" Her voice was thick with sleep, and suddenly I realized why.

"Miss, I'm so sorry. I forgot about the time difference." I did a quick mental calculation; it was somewhere around two in the morning back in Kansas City. "I'll call you back later."

I started to flip my phone closed, but then I heard her voice calling my name.

"Claire? Claire! No. Don't hang up."

She sounded a little more awake now. Awake and concerned. "What's wrong?"

If ever I needed a listening ear, this was the moment, but now I couldn't dump all my troubles on Missy. Even under the best of circumstances, I had difficulty sharing my feelings with other people. "Look, go back to sleep. I'll call you after lunch or something."

"Don't hang up!" I could hear her scrambling to sit up. Phillip mumbled sleepily in the background. "Talk to me, Claire."

Those simple words set loose a torrent of tears on my end of the line. I snuffled and snorted and generally fell apart, while Missy made soothing noises from thousands of miles away.

"It's okay, honey. Whatever it is, we'll figure it out." Missy crooned the words in my ear.

I'd never been on the receiving end of them before, and unfortunately they just made me cry harder. I indulged myself for about five dollars' worth of transatlantic tear time before I set the phone down on the bench beside me and reached into my purse for some tissues. After blowing my nose several times, I picked the phone back up.

"Sorry."

"Would you quit apologizing?" Missy's irritation was obvious. "Look, tell me what's going on."

"I've ruined everything." I pinched the bridge of my nose in hopes that it would stop any further tears.

"Claire—"

"It's true. I've been living my life for other people for so long, and what have I got to show for it? No job. No boyfriend. And cows for an alarm clock."

"What? Wait."

But I didn't. I rambled on, unable to stop myself now that the dam had burst.

"Everything I do is for other people, and why? Where has it gotten me?"

"Would you please tell me what in the world you're talking about?"

"I have to stop, Missy. I have to stop taking care of you." My internal censor had apparently deserted me, because words started pouring out of my mouth that I might have thought for a long time but would never have dreamed of saying aloud.

"Well, finally," Missy said.

"Finally?" I squeaked. I had to tighten my jaw so it wouldn't drop too far. "Finally?" I swallowed back fresh tears. "After everything I've done for you and the kids and Phil, you'd say that?"

Images flashed in front of me. Sewing the kids' Halloween costumes well into the early morning hours. Picking up Phillip from the airport at every hour of the day and night to save him the cost of a cab. Helping Missy set up her classroom every fall. "Are you saying the fact that you used me all these years is my fault?"

I could hear Missy's sigh of exasperation as clearly as if she'd been sitting next to me.

"Nobody gets used unless they want to, Claire," she said. "We were just trying to fill the void for you."

"The void?" Had I stepped into some sort of evil parallel universe where suddenly Missy was the competent sister and I was, in fact, the dependent one?

"You've never managed to build a life of your own," she went on. "That's why I was so happy you could go in my place to Oxford. I thought it might be a fresh start."

Anger exploded in my chest, sharp and fierce with deadly claws. "I have to go. I'll talk to you later."

"Claire—"

I pushed the red button on my cell phone and snapped it shut. More tears burst forth, and I couldn't control them. I didn't want to control them. All those years. All that effort. For what? For ingratitude and blame?

"Here."

A tissue appeared in front of me. A tissue attached to a masculine hand. Which was attached to the forearm I'd lately come to find so compelling.

My head jerked up, shock and disbelief warring with my grief. "What are you doing here?"

Neil slid onto the bench beside me. The warm sunshine, the beauty of the flowers, the soft whisper of the breeze—none of it mattered. Because my life had just been stripped of all its meaning. Everything I'd believed, everything I'd built my life on, had never really existed. At least, not outside my own head.

Missy felt sorry for me. That, more than anything, devastated me.

"I'm an idiot," I mumbled in between sniffs. I wiped my nose with the tissue.

"No, you're not." He reached over and laid his hand on my knee. "Misguided, maybe, but definitely not an idiot."

"Why are you here? What about your plane?" I kept my

gaze focused on the grass at my feet since I couldn't bring myself to look him in the eye.

His arm stiffened. "Do you want me to leave?"

"No," I said, alarmed that he'd misunderstood. "No, that's not what I meant." How could I even begin to explain to him what I did mean?

"It's just as if everything I always thought…everything I counted on…none of it was real. It's gone."

"Just like your parents."

My head snapped up, and now I did look him in the eye. He was watching me with kindness and compassion and all the things I'd taken for granted from him.

"It's not like that." But it was. I knew it. My body knew it, which was why I was shaking so hard. "It can't be like that."

"Why can't it be?" He asked the question tenderly. Lovingly. His voice made me ache.

"Because I can't survive it again, Neil. I can't."

I threw myself against his chest, no easy feat given that we were sitting side by side. I was too distraught to care about the complexities and nuances of our relationship. No, I was like a child all over again. It was what I had been, really, when my parents died. I'd only been eighteen years old. I might have been an adult legally, but I'd been so close to my mother and father. Had depended on them so much. Probably too much. And then they'd been taken away from me in an instant, and the only thing I'd known to do was to try and be my parents for Missy.

Or had it been for Missy?

Her words had lodged uncomfortably in the region of my heart. Had I really done it for my sister's sake? Sacrificed my dreams and plans just so she could have a home? Or had I, in fact, only done it for me, just as she'd said?

"It's okay," he murmured against my hair, his arms wrapped around me. "It'll be okay."

In that moment, I wished so keenly that I had that engagement ring on my finger that it hurt. The enormity of what I'd done and of what I now understood about my feelings for Neil pressed against my chest.

I pulled back from his embrace, and he let me go. The tissue, now soaked beyond any usefulness, was still clutched in my hand.

"Sorry I didn't bring more of those," he said.

"I'm sure you didn't expect me to fall apart again." I paused to dab at my eyes. "It's becoming a habit."

He didn't respond. He just sat quietly beside me as I turned away from him and faced the beautiful prospect of the Master's Garden again.

Once upon a time, I'd thought if only my life had been different, if my parents hadn't died, I would have had everything I ever wanted. Now I was ready to admit that no one ever got everything they wanted. If they did, it often turned out to be something that they didn't really desire after all.

"Why didn't you get on the plane?" I asked again, this time in slightly better shape to hear the answer.

"I couldn't."

"Why not?"

He laughed, but not in a happy way. "I left my passport in the nightstand drawer in my hotel room."

My heart sank so low I thought I might see it on the impeccably manicured lawn at my feet. "Did you find it?"

"They were holding it at the front desk. But by the time I took the bus back here, I was too late to get to the airport again and make the flight. So I stayed another night."

"Have you rebooked already?" Even though I was so deeply glad he was sitting next to me, I desperately wanted him gone. Because that's what he wanted. And because I was a complete and total idiot. I had gone and fallen in love with my own boyfriend, only now he wasn't my boyfriend anymore.

"The airline's working on it," he said, and I ignored the pain that gripped my midsection.

So he was still leaving. And my ring finger was still bare. And James wasn't my Mr. Darcy at all. No, the man sitting beside me, the man who'd stood by me through thick and thin, who'd tolerated my codependence on my sister, who had confessed to taking me for granted, who had waited so patiently for me to see the light—he was the hero I'd been waiting for all my life. But I'd been too blind to see that what mattered at the end of the day, or at the end of a lifetime, was not how handsome a man was or how rich or powerful. Or even how smitten a man was with you. What mattered was whether he was the kind of man who would stand by you, whatever happened. What mattered was whether he was the kind of man who would make sacrifices for you, and for whom you would gladly make your own sacrifices.

"Neil, I don't know what—"

He pulled away from me. I bit back a small cry of protest.

"I just wanted to say good-bye the right way." He reached out and tapped the end of my nose. A nose that I was sure must be red, swollen, and not the least bit attractive.

"We had a good run, Claire. No hard feelings, okay?"

A good run? No hard feelings? What were we, a NASCAR race?

"No, of course not."

He stood up and then looked down at me with sympathy. "I'm sure you and Missy will sort this out. It's just a sister thing."

I nodded. "Of course. You're right."

He was completely wrong. It wasn't a sister thing at all. It was a *me* thing. Or, more to the point, a "What's wrong with me?" thing.

He glanced at his watch. "Look, I'm going to have to go. My cab's waiting. I just didn't want to leave it like… Well, I just wanted to say good-bye the right way."

How can there be a right way to say good-bye to someone you love?

That was what I wanted to say, but I didn't. Instead, I gave him a watery smile.

"Mission accomplished."

He frowned. "You're sure? I can send the cab away."

I shook my head vigorously. "No, Neil. There's no reason for you to stay."

Other than that I love you.

"All right." He paused. "We can still be friends, right? I mean, just because you and I didn't work out—"

"Sure." I stood up too and pasted the biggest fake smile in the history of womankind on my face. "Friends. Absolutely. Always."

"Great. That's great, then." But he didn't look that pleased, really. He stood there for a long time. Looking at me. Not saying anything. And then, finally, he spoke. "We'll go to a Royals game or something. When you get back."

"Okay."

I knew what that meant. It meant that I was never going to see him again.

"Good-bye, Claire." He leaned over and pressed a kiss against my cheek. I resisted the ferocious need to throw my arms around him and keep him from leaving.

"Bye, Neil." Breathe, I reminded myself. Just keep breathing.

He hesitated, and then he reached into his pocket and pulled out that blue velvet box. "I want you to keep this."

"No, I couldn't—"

He pressed the box into my hand. "I can't return it. And I couldn't give it to anyone else. Maybe you can have it made into a necklace or something."

"Or something." I bit my lip so I wouldn't burst into tears.

"Good-bye, Claire." He turned and walked away across the beautifully manicured lawn. My last sight of him was as he disappeared through the gate, and I was left alone in the Master's Garden, as if he'd never been there at all.

fter Neil left me alone in the garden, I cried for a long time. But something about those tears cleansed me. By the time I finished, I only had a few minutes to get to the last seminar. Although I was heartsick and exhausted, I decided I didn't want to miss the final session.

Martin was the last to present. I took a seat next to him and avoided looking at James. Eleanor called the group to order, and we began.

"What I have admired about Jane Austen's work," Martin said, speaking without any notes, "is the quiet courage of her characters. They are not prime ministers or princesses but ordinary people. Her heroines, in particular, must be strong because they are so often at a disadvantage, either because of their financial situation or because of their families."

I found myself nodding in agreement. Although the occasional character might be wealthy—Darcy and Bingley being the prime examples—most of the people in Austen's work were reflections of the gentry and working classes she had known in her life.

"The word *courage*, of course, comes from the French word *coeur*, or heart in English," Martin continued. "Austen shows us that it is in knowing one's heart that one may find the courage to overcome obstacles. One of Elizabeth Bennet's obstacles is her prejudice against Mr. Darcy, but another is the belief that she is somewhat better than her neighbors or her sisters. In her own way, she is as proud as Mr. Darcy. But over the course of the novel, she must learn that she is as human—and as subject to errors in judgment—as anyone else."

Even Eleanor was nodding in agreement.

"Real courage, Austen shows us, is not in overcoming external threats or forces. No, the most difficult kind of courage is the kind we must find to know and understand our own hearts." Martin paused and looked around the circle, but his gaze stopped when it came to me.

I nodded with understanding.

So many of the circumstances of my life were beyond my control. I couldn't bring back my parents. I couldn't even get back my job or my boyfriend. But Martin was telling me that somewhere inside of me was everything I needed to face the ruins of my life and start to rebuild it.

Honestly. Imperfectly. So that my life would be mine, and not an accommodation of other people's needs and wishes. No wonder I hadn't been able to get my relationship with Neil right. How could he have truly known me when I hadn't even known myself?

Martin crossed his arms over his chest. "That's all I have to say."

For a long moment, the room was quiet, and then Rosie and Louise burst into applause. The others followed, including me. Even Eleanor. I didn't think that even Jane Austen herself could have said it any better.

❧❧❧❧❧

Eleanor devoted the second half of the morning to another general discussion of Austen and what we'd learned that week.

"I think you can see how complex any issue surrounding Jane Austen becomes," Eleanor was saying, "especially given her popularity. Film and television adaptations tend to blur our understanding, enjoyable as they may be. No, it's only when we go back to the page, to her very words, that we may find insight into her work."

The week has seemed both eternal and fleeting, I thought, as we stood to exchange our good-byes. I hugged Martin as well as Rosie and Louise, shook hands with Olga and the cardiologist, and then found myself standing awkwardly in front of James. What in the world could I say to him in the midst of all those people?

"Claire." He stood there, looking solemn.

"James." I took a deep breath. "It's been—" What? Nice to meet you? Tons of fun? Ultimate agony?

"Will you go outside with me?" he asked. "We need to talk."

He had a strange look on his face, as if he'd eaten something very wrong for breakfast. I glanced around. The others were caught up in conversation as they said their farewells and exchanged e-mail addresses.

"Um, sure. I guess."

I followed him out of the seminar room and down the stairs until we emerged into Tom Quad. He walked a little way down the cloister and then stopped.

"Claire, I owe you an apology."

I'd been studying the straps on my sandals, but his words made my gaze shoot back up to his face.

"You? Owe *me* an apology?" Even after everything that had happened, he still made me blush like a schoolgirl. "I don't think so, James. I think it's the other way around."

He reached out and took my hand in his. That was the last thing I would have expected him to do. But even though I still found him incredibly handsome, I didn't feel a single zing at his touch.

"Claire, I need to make a confession of my own."

"Oh?" Whatever it was, he could hardly top me in the duplicity department.

"It's about Jane Austen."

"What?"

Now his cheeks were tinged with red, and he shifted his weight from one foot to the other.

I understood then. Maybe he really was a Jane Austen fan after all, a big, goopy romantic, but he'd been too ashamed, too worried about his reputation or his manliness to own up to the truth.

"It's okay, James. A lot of guys like Jane Austen. I mean, look at Martin."

"No, that's not what I mean."

Now I was confused. "What do you mean?"

I could hear the other seminar participants pounding down the staircase in the building behind us. Whatever James needed to say, I realized he'd better say it fast if we were to have any privacy.

"I didn't pursue you because I was romantically interested in you." I could see the muscle in his jaw strained tight with tension.

"But you asked me out," I said. "And that kiss—"

His fingers tightened around mine. "I was using you."

"What?"

His shoulders slumped. "I pursued you only after I found out about your friendship with Harriet."

Whatever I had expected him to say, that certainly wasn't it. "I don't understand."

The others were almost at the doorway. James pulled me a little farther along the walk.

"I thought you would be the easiest way to get to the manuscript."

"The manuscript?" It was almost as if he were speaking to me in a foreign language.

He put his hand over his mouth and chin and then wiped downward as if he thought he could wipe away his words as well. "Harriet's manuscript." He said the last word as if it were poison.

And then I understood. "You want to publish it."

"I thought I'd hit the jackpot. Eleanor went to school with an editor who works for me. He was visiting her here, and she had a little too much to drink and spilled the beans. Once Oliver told me about the manuscript, I knew we'd struck gold. Eleanor tried to get it from her mother, but she wasn't having any luck. I signed up for the seminar to see if I could get anywhere with Harriet. Then you waltzed in, and she was practically shoving it into your hands."

"And I was an easy mark." A strange tingling crept through my limbs, and humiliation poured in after it. I had been conned. Completely and utterly tricked. A handsome face, a little bit of attention, and I had been putty in his hands.

"It was you, wasn't it, who broke into my room?" I had suspected Mrs. Parrot, but it had never occurred to me that the intruder might have been James.

"You should hate me," he was saying. "I won't blame you if you do."

"Why are you telling me this now?" I wanted to sink through the paving stones beneath my feet. I was an even bigger idiot than I'd thought, not to have seen through him. I wanted to melt into the earth and never see the light of day again.

He dropped his grasp on my fingers. "I thought you deserved to know the truth. Especially after what happened with—what was his name?"

"Neil," I supplied automatically.

"With Neil." He paused. Now James looked even more serious than he had to begin with. His dark eyes had gone almost black.

"What?" I wasn't sure I could stand any more revelations. I'd had too many shocks to my system already.

"Well, the other part of the truth is that"—he looked me squarely in the eye—"whatever my intentions were at the start, somewhere along the way, well..." He drew a deep breath. "The truth is that somewhere along the way, I fell for you."

As little as forty-eight hours earlier, those words would have thrilled me beyond human comprehension. Now I simply found them depressing. Yes, I was flattered. But I was also aware of just what an idiot I had been over a man I barely knew, and I was also aware of just how much that idiocy had cost me.

"I just wanted you to know," James said.

Was he trying to start something again? I couldn't tell from the granitelike set of his jaw.

"Thank you," I said, unsure of what else to say. "For telling me."

"If you thought you could forgive me..." He trailed off, a hopeful expression in his eyes, but I shook my head.

"It's over, James."

He shrugged. "Okay. I have to respect that."

"Yes. You do."

He reached out and squeezed my shoulder. "Take care. I hope you find the right person for you."

"Yeah. You too," I said.

I watched him walk away, but I felt none of the pain I'd experienced as I'd watched Neil leave. Amazing how twenty-four hours could change a person so completely, and how completely a person's feelings could change in that same amount of time.

"I hope I find someone too," I said to the back of James's head as he disappeared from sight.

❧❧❧❧❧

I wanted to forget everything that had happened in the past week, but something Eleanor said that morning stuck in my head. To find insight into Austen's work, she said, go back to the page. And I realized that if I ever wanted to know the truth about what might have changed between Austen's first version of *Pride and Prejudice* and the final one, I was in the perfect place to find out.

I remembered from the *Joining Notes* that one of our privileges as seminar participants was access to the reading rooms at the Bodleian Library. I made my way to Broad Street and found the entrance. From there I found several helpful librarians who submitted a request for the books I needed and then helped me settle into the Lower Camera Reading Room.

While I waited for the books to be pulled from the stacks and sent up, I gazed around the circular room and looked wistfully at the packed shelves, the students bent over their work, the atmosphere of academic pursuit. I'd never known that kind of life and always felt I was missing something.

But an hour and several Jane Austen biographies later, I wasn't sure I was cut out for scholarly efforts. My head swam with dates and descriptions and differing accounts. I'd scribbled notes on the tiny pieces of paper provided, and as I looked back through them, I thought they seemed like pieces of a puzzle that was eluding me.

Martin was right. A lot had occurred in Austen's life in the years after *First Impressions*. Tom Lefroy's return to the neighborhood and his failure to pay a call on the Austens. Her father's retirement and their removal to Bath. Then her father's death and a long, unsettled period when Austen and her sisters lived with various of the brothers or occasionally in rented lodgings. Years without any new writing. And finally, happily, a more permanent home in a cottage near their brother Edward's home at Chawton. It was there that she began to revise her earlier work.

But did any of what I'd read really have to do with the differences between *First Impressions* and *Pride and Prejudice*? Could it account for the very different Darcys?

And then as I moved the little slips of paper around on the desk in front of me, arranging them and rearranging them in hopes of making sense of it all, I caught a glimmer of an answer. A small window into another woman's soul. And perhaps a peek into my own as well. I saw the truth about Fitzwilliam Darcy, and the effect of loss and the passage of time on a woman's ability to love. I saw why Jane Austen had changed her mind, and I respected her all the more for it.

fled the Bodleian Library, clutching those slips of paper, and raced down the river path to Harriet's cottage. The rain the night before had broken the grip of the punishing heat wave, and now Oxford lay in warm, but not stifling, summer stillness.

Harriet was as glad to see me as always, and I felt a pang as I followed her into the sitting room.

"No tea today," she said and waved a hand at the tray on the low table in front of the sofa. It contained a bottle of sherry and two glasses. "Today, we celebrate."

"Yes, we can, but I needed to—"

"Catch your breath, dear. Really, we've all the time in the world."

"Yes, but Harriet—"

"One thing at a time, Claire. One thing at a time."

My smile must have been pretty weak, because she leaned over to pat my arm. "Cheer up, dear. I have a very good feeling about today."

I was glad that one of us did.

"I don't want to say good-bye to you," I said, my throat tight. "You've been the best part of the week."

She laughed and reached to pour the sherry. "That's not what Eleanor tells me."

So Harriet did know about my romantic drama. She handed me a glass, the amber liquid catching the light from the window like a jewel.

"How are you? Really?" she asked, before taking a sip from her own glass.

I hadn't planned on telling her everything that had happened, but as it turned out, I did. She cooed and sympathized and poured me more sherry. Half an hour later, I was feeling decidedly better, if a little woozy.

"So your young man has gone home, and now you're seeing this James more like the original Mr. Darcy." She made a clucking noise like a mother hen. "You've had quite a trying week, haven't you? And I suppose I haven't really helped."

I opened my mouth to protest, but she ignored me and rose from the sofa. I wanted to make sense of it all. I wanted to keep talking about it until an answer became clear.

"I spent some time at the Bodleian. I wanted to know more about Jane Austen. To try and understand her."

Harriet looked at me with pleasure. "An excellent idea. A lovely place, too, for finding answers. Almost as good as my cottage," she said with a teasing smile. "Tell me what you learned."

"I'm sure you already know what happened," I said.

"Yes, but tell me your interpretation."

I drew a deep breath. "She learned the full effects of being a woman with no financial means. I always thought she must have been quite wealthy from her writing, but she barely made any money at all."

"Yes. Very different from what would have happened if she'd been alive today."

"And she and Cassandra were so dependent on their brothers' whims. As was their mother. Of course, it probably never occurred to the men in the family that their female relations would have liked a home of their own. A permanent home." I paused, considering the thought. "It was only when Jane had finally settled down that she could really do the work she was meant to do."

"The place was important, yes," Harriet said, "but I think she must have finally decided that she would work on her writing no matter what happened."

"Have you been there? To Chawton?"

"A long time ago." Harriet's eyes grew misty. "I remember being quite moved. I could just picture her at her little writing table by the window, pulling *First Impressions* out from some hiding place and beginning to rework it."

"I do think she started the book because of Tom Lefroy. Originally, I mean."

"Her most famous flirtation," Harriet said with a smile.

"Yes. I can't tell that she really loved him, but he certainly seems to have inspired Mr. Darcy."

Harriet nodded. "What else did you learn?"

I thought about what I'd read at the library. "I would imagine that ten years later, her perspective on Mr. Lefroy might have undergone some changes. I think she became a little more understanding of his family's concern over the affair and why he never came to see her again."

"Do you think he was the love of her life?" Harriet asked.

I shook my head. "No. I think he could have been, if circumstances had been different."

"If one of them had been rich, you mean," Harriet said with a twinkle in her eye.

"Among other things."

I sipped my sherry and Harriet leaned forward. "Is finding the right person just a matter of luck, then?" she asked.

I shrugged. "Perhaps. But I think there's something sort of…divine going on as well."

"Divine?"

"A purpose. Some unseen hand. That sort of thing." I wasn't sure what I was trying to say exactly.

"Do you think that's what Austen was doing when she rewrote the book? Playing God?"

I shook my head. "I don't know that she was playing God. Maybe she was more inclined to hope, after she had grown up. To see the possibility of redemption in a hero who'd fallen short."

Harriet smiled. "I have something else for you to read."

She crossed to her usual chair, the one in front of the

window. I hadn't noticed before, but there was something in it. Something flat, tied with a red ribbon.

"I'd forgotten about the old trunks in the attic, you see. Spent most of yesterday going through them, one by one, but it was worth it in the end."

She returned and laid the bundle in my lap.

By now I had no trouble recognizing Jane Austen's handwriting. And even if I hadn't, the familiar aged look of the paper would have told me everything I needed to know.

She smiled at me. "This is definitely the last bit. But I think you'll find it was worth the wait."

My heartbeat picked up its pace. "May I read it right now?"

Harriet chuckled. "Of course, dear. Of course."

First Impressions
Chapter Twenty

Mr. and Mrs. Gardiner's house in Gracechurch Street, Cheapside, was respectable enough but far from the fashionable part of London. Elizabeth rejoiced in that distance, for she might rest secure in the knowledge that she would never encounter any of the Rosings party when she and Jane were abroad on errands for their aunt. She did admit to some trepidation when they ventured into Bond Street on a commission to the drapers' shop Mrs. Gardiner favored, but they returned unscathed. London, to be sure, was a very large place, and one might remain there in anonymity for weeks on end.

Elizabeth took great pleasure in every hour of the days she spent with her older sister, for they were fleeting. After a fortnight's respite, she found herself ready to book passage on the mail coach to Brighton. Her mother's letters, which had begun to flow in an unceasing stream when news of Elizabeth's disgrace reached her, would only be stopped by her quitting London and arriving in Brighton to tell all.

But what could she tell her mother? Certainly not the truth.

She and Jane were spending the morning, her last in London, doing such mending as might be necessary for her journey. Mr. Gardiner's sitting room faced east, and so the light proved excellent for any work involving needle and thread. Their aunt had excused herself to settle a crisis with the cook, and the Gardiner children were ensconced in the nursery under the good offices of two of the housemaids.

"I wish you would stay," Jane said as she plied her needle in an attempt to salvage a well-worn stocking. "You are not yourself, Lizzie. Mama will understand." She said the last bit with less conviction than she'd shown with the first.

"You know I cannot. I have presented myself at the employment agencies here. Something will turn up soon, I am sure. I can read their letters as easily in Brighton as in London. In the meantime, one of us must make certain that Lydia has not twisted Mama completely around her finger."

"But—"

Jane was interrupted by a knock at the front door. The two sisters sat, listening with great interest, while Mr. Gardiner's man answered the summons. A masculine voice was heard in the hallway, and then Simmons, the manservant, opened the sitting-room door. He bowed to Elizabeth.

"A gentleman, ma'am, for you, Miss Elizabeth."

"A gentleman?" *Jane dropped her needlework into her lap.* "Pray, who is it, Simmons?"

Elizabeth feared she knew, but she schooled her features into calm regularity. She would not panic. Neither would she tremble.

"A Colonel Fitzwilliam, ma'am."

Elizabeth shot up from the sofa. "What?"

Jane's hand reached out to pull her back down. "Mr. Darcy's cousin, Lizzie? But why?"

Elizabeth regained her composure as quickly as she had relinquished it. "Please show him in, Simmons." *She rose again from the sofa, but slowly this time, and Jane with her. They faced the door, and Elizabeth's pulse drummed in her throat as if the colonel had come to bid her march with his regiment.*

And then he was there, framed in the doorway. He wore a morning coat of blue superfine, and the leather of his Hessians gleamed with polish.

"Miss Bennet," *he said with a bow to Jane.* "Miss Elizabeth."

"Colonel Fitzwilliam." *Elizabeth stepped forward*

and made a curtsy. "Please allow me to present you to my sister Jane."

The two exchanged pleasantries, which gave Elizabeth a moment to settle her thoughts, if not her feelings.

"I am sorry to impose upon you, Miss Bennet," he said to Jane, "but I had urgent business in town and did not have time to send a note. Thank you for your patience."

Jane looked bewildered but beautiful as always. "Certainly, Colonel. Pray, tell us, how may we be of assistance to you?"

The colonel hesitated for a moment and then took a deep breath, as if to fortify himself for battle. "Miss Bennet," he said to Jane, "might I have a word with your sister?"

Jane smothered a smile and cast a reproving glance at Elizabeth. "Colonel, it is not at all the thing—"

"We shall leave the door ajar," he said, his expression very grave indeed. "Perhaps you would be so good as to stand just outside?" He paused. "In case your sister has need of you?"

What he meant, of course, was in case anyone should happen along. Then Jane might slip back into the room, and Elizabeth's reputation would be saved.

Elizabeth, however, was not in support of such a scheme. "No, Jane. That will not be necessary."

But her words had little effect on her sister. "Five minutes, Colonel," Jane said with her gentle smile. "And not a moment more."

"Jane—" Elizabeth's protest was in vain. Her sister

disappeared from the room, leaving the door ajar as the colonel had suggested. "Sir—"

"You have no wish to see me, I'm sure," he said, stepping toward her. Elizabeth resisted the impulse to retreat. "But I knew that I must come."

"You have no right, sir, to cut up my peace in this manner. Surely you have done enough already."

The censure in her words might have appeared directed at the colonel, but in truth, it was only for herself. He had done as honor dictated when she had made the fatal mistake of confessing the truth of Mr. Darcy's feelings to him.

I looked up at Harriet, who was still on the sofa next to me. "She told the colonel about Mr. Darcy's near-proposal? But why?"

Harriet shrugged. "I have no idea. Perhaps she felt guilty or needed a listening ear."

"And the colonel blew the whistle. Just in case his cousin succumbed to Elizabeth's charms after all."

"Apparently. Although I'm sure Lady Catherine laid the blame at Elizabeth's feet."

"No wonder she fled to London in disgrace. But not before Lady Catherine fired her."

"I would imagine Lady Catherine took issue with what she believed to be Elizabeth's scheming after a rich husband."

I laughed. "Yes, I suppose she did. But why did the colonel come to London?"

Harriet pointed toward the page. "Keep reading, dear."

Elizabeth frowned at the colonel. "Why are you here, sir? I have complied with your wishes. Your cousin is safe from my grasp. All is well at Rosings."

Colonel Fitzwilliam clasped his hands behind his back, as if preparing to review the troops. "There you are quite wrong, ma'am. Yes, most of the party at Rosings are quite recovered. But there is one person who is in a very bad way. A very bad way, indeed."

Elizabeth had not succumbed to her feelings from the moment she had departed Rosings. And now, in her uncle's morning room, the colonel standing tall and imposing in front of her, she felt her composure began to weaken.

"I hope you do not mean Miss de Bourgh. She was very well when I left her."

"She was in tears and very angry with her mother. Your company meant a great deal to her."

"I am sorry to cause her distress."

He cleared his throat. "But it was not Miss de Bourgh of whom I was speaking."

Elizabeth had turned to examine a china figurine on the mantelpiece, but at his words, she faced him again. "Was it not?"

He reached out and took her hand in his. "Elizabeth—" His voice grew thick with emotion. "We have very little time. Let us speak plainly with one another."

"You made your feelings about me quite clear, Colonel, when you informed your aunt that your cousin was in peril. You need not have troubled yourself to come all this way."

He lifted her hand, brought it to his lips, and pressed a kiss against it. Elizabeth was so startled that she forgot, for one long moment, to breathe. A sudden weakness in her knees and the very real possibility of fainting brought her to her senses.

"Sir—"

"I am no Darcy," the colonel said, his eyes dark with feeling. "I have no Pemberley, madam, and nothing like his twenty thousand pounds per annum."

Heat rose in Elizabeth's cheeks. "I am no fortune hunter, sir," she said. "Whatever you may think."

He shook his head. "No, you are not. I never said you were, however my aunt might have represented my actions." He paused, and then to Elizabeth's alarm, he lowered himself to one knee. He was still in possession of her hand, and she knew, in that moment, that he was truly in possession of her heart.

"Colonel—"

"Dearest, loveliest Elizabeth. My motives in exposing my cousin's attachment to you were entirely selfish."

"Sir, please, do not—"

"I will. I must." He pressed his lips to her hand once more. "Darcy might have fancied himself in love with you, but he did not love you enough to risk the censure of his family and friends. I have no such hesitation. Refuse me, if you will. But I must ask. Will you marry me, Elizabeth? Will you make me the happiest of men?"

She knew she should refuse, for his sake, no matter what her own feelings might be. "I am a very bad bargain, sir. I come with a large number of encumbrances. Five of them to be exact. All female and all sure to plague you for the rest of your days."

He rose to stand beside her then and took her other hand in his. "I shall not mind," he said, leaning toward her, "as long as you will agree to plague me as well."

Jane, who had stood all this time with her ear pressed to the door, knew that the requisite five minutes had expired, but she made no move to open the door and reenter the room. In truth, it was only when Mrs. Gardiner appeared at the landing on the stairs above that Jane greeted her brightly enough to warn the pair inside the morning room and then entered herself, eager to wish her sister happy.

Much later, after the colonel and Mr. Gardiner had met in private in the latter gentleman's library, and a toast to the happy couple had been drunk, Colonel Fitzwilliam mentioned another matter of business he hoped to conduct while in town.

"My cousin, Mr. Darcy, has charged me to deliver a message to his friend Mr. Bingley. He is a gentleman of wealth but no property and has long been searching for an appropriate situation."

"Mr. Bingley?" Elizabeth said. "We have heard of him. I believe he once expressed an interest in Netherfield Park."

"Yes," said Jane with a smile. "It was a great disappointment to the neighborhood when he did not settle there."

"You must come accompany me when I call on him," Colonel Fitzwilliam said to Jane and Elizabeth. "You will like Bingley well enough, I am sure. He is always a great favorite."

"We are always glad of a new acquaintance," Jane said and reached to pour the colonel another cup of tea.

I set the last page on the sofa table and allowed the mixture of feelings—joy, frustration, sadness—to wash over me. Lizzie married Colonel Fitzwilliam after Darcy spurned her. So that was it, then. *First Impressions.* Not the equal to *Pride and Prejudice*, but a small jewel in its own way, and perhaps a guide for how I might mend my own life. Perhaps the hero wasn't born, but made. And perhaps a true heroine learned the difference only by having her heart broken along the way.

"Harriet…" I spread my hand across the pages, as if seeking answers by touch rather than reason. But then I stopped. Because in that moment, the answers became clear. "I know what you should do with the manuscript."

She leaned forward. "Yes? What would your advice be, then, dear?"

And so I told her.

❧❧❧❧❧❧

I was walking home from the cottage when my cell phone rang. To my surprise, it was Missy.

"How are you?" she said. "I kept thinking you would call me back. I've been worried."

"I'm fine. Just exhausted. And confused. And worried. And—"

Missy laughed.

"What?" I couldn't hide my annoyance.

"I'm sorry, but for the first time in a long time, you sound like a normal human being."

"Thanks a lot." My fingers closed around the phone. "I appreciate your vote of confidence."

"I'm just saying that it's okay for you to be human. To make mistakes. To make a mess or two."

My spine stiffened. "Believe me, I've made plenty of mistakes."

"It's not making them that's your problem," Missy said. "It's admitting to them. You've buried yourself so deep in responsibility that I don't know how you ever breathe."

"I do not—"

"You didn't die with them."

I jerked back from the phone, stung. "That's a horrible thing to say. I know that. Don't patronize—"

"But that's how you've lived your life ever since Mom and Dad were killed. As if you didn't exist anymore. Or only existed to protect me."

"But—"

"It's time, Claire. Time for you to pick up the pieces and move forward."

"I thought that was what I've been doing." Even though I recognized the truth in her words and had even said similar things to myself in the past few days, it was still painful to hear them coming from someone else.

"I'm okay now, Claire." She chuckled ruefully. "Well, as okay as I'm ever going to get in the midst of this craziness."

As if on cue, I could hear my nieces run screaming through the room past Missy. "Jocelyn! Slow down!" Missy called after her for all the good it did.

I could picture it all in my mind. The twins racing through the family room, the big Lab hot on their heels and barking for all he was worth. Even knowing how chaotic my sister's life could be, I saw in that moment that she was right. Did she need a maid? Yes. An au pair? Definitely. Me running her life and rescuing her from every hint of danger? No. Not anymore.

I should have felt jubilant at this confirmation of what I'd so recently realized. I should have felt liberated. Free at last. But all I felt was deeply sad. Neil had been right after all. He'd said that one day I would wake up and discover that I had no life of my own. And that day was today.

"Claire? It's going to be okay, you know."

That was the final nail in the coffin, her reaching out to comfort me as I had reached out to her all those years ago. The tables were now well and fully turned.

"I'm okay," I said. I refused to cry. "At least, I will be."

"What are you going to do when you get back? You know you're welcome to stay with us if you need to give up your apartment."

I shook my head, even though she couldn't see me from an ocean away. "I'll be fine. I'll find a cheaper apartment. An efficiency. Something simple. And then"—I took a deep breath—"I think I'm going to register for college at KU starting in the fall."

And then I could hear Missy crying on the other end of the line.

"It's okay, sis." I made the same soothing noises she'd been making a few moments before. "I wouldn't change a thing, even if I could. But you're right. It's time for a fresh start. Time to do something for myself. And the first thing I want to do is get my degree."

"What will you major in?" I could hear her sniffing back her tears.

Suddenly I felt as if a great weight had tumbled from my shoulders. "I have absolutely no idea. That's the best part. I'm going to take whatever strikes my fancy until, well, until I figure out what strikes my fancy."

"Including a Jane Austen seminar or two?" Missy asked with a laugh.

Despite everything that had happened, I could laugh along with her. "Yeah. Maybe. Only nothing that includes *Pride and Prejudice* in any form or fashion."

I thought about how excited Missy would have been to be

invited into Harriet Dalrymple's cottage to read the manuscript to which I'd been privy. I hated keeping such an enormous secret from my sister, but I had promised.

"What about Neil?" Missy asked. "Have you talked to him
since he left?"

"I don't think he's interested in being part of my new life.
Not after everything that's happened."

"But isn't he worth fighting for? Shouldn't you at least try
to see him?"

"I don't think so." He'd made his feelings about our lack
of a future clear during that last conversation.

"What if you—"

"Missy, stop. Don't worry about me. I'll be okay."

"I know you will. But I'd like for you to be happy as well
as okay."

Now tears were filling my eyes too, and I knew it was time
to hang up. "I'll see you soon."

"Yeah. See you soon."

I snapped my phone shut and stowed it in my purse.

arriet had asked me to do one last thing for her, and so on Saturday morning, I entered the courtyard of the Bodleian Library with both trepidation and relief. This time, though, I wasn't there to do research. This time I was on an errand of a very different nature, one that would surely make the librarians of that great library expire on the spot, if they knew of it.

I had once more tucked the manuscript of *First Impressions* in my purse, and the weight of it, both physically and emotionally, hung heavy on my shoulder. The courtyard would be busier later in the day, as students and tourists began moving about, but at the moment, it was fairly quiet. I stood uncomfortably, shifting from one foot to the other, eager to complete my task. Several long minutes passed before I saw her, framed in the archway. She paused when she saw me and then moved forward with purpose.

"Good morning, Miss Prescott."

"Good morning, Mrs. Parrot."

She wore a heavy cardigan over another flowered dress and carried a black umbrella that looked to have weathered a number of storms.

"Harriet called and asked that I meet you here, but she wouldn't say why." The older woman held herself stiffly, as if bracing for bad news. "Although perhaps I can guess. She's given you the manuscript, hasn't she?"

I slipped my purse from my shoulder and reached inside. Harriet had tied the pages together with another piece of ribbon, lavender this time. "Yes. She gave it to me." I held it front of me, testing the weight of it in my hands.

Mrs. Parrot's shoulders sank. "I had hoped—" She broke off in midsentence, as if overcome, but then she took a deep breath and straightened her spine. "I have no choice except to respect Harriet's wishes, but if there is any way I can persuade you to reconsider…" She shook her head. "But you know the value of the manuscript, of course. I am sure your friend, Mr. Beaufort, will be happy to help you squeeze every shilling from it."

"Mrs. Parrot—"

"You need not say anything else." She tucked her umbrella under her arm, as if sheathing a sword. "Although I would ask you, please, not to say anything of the Formidables. Allow the manuscript to be enough."

"But, Mrs. Parrot—"

"The hunt will be on, of course, once this turns up, for all things Austen. We will need to redouble our efforts." She pinned me with her gaze. "I hope it will be worth it. At least reassure me you will see to Harriet's comfort with the proceeds."

"Mrs. Parrot, please." I held up my free hand. "If you would let me get a word in edgewise…"

Her jaw dropped. "Edgewise? My good woman—"

"I'm giving you the manuscript," I blurted out. "Harriet asked me what she should do, and I told her she should give you the manuscript."

"What?" She looked as if I'd just struck her.

"She wants the Formidables to have it. I told her that it was the right thing to do."

I had expected Mrs. Parrot to receive the news with some joy. Instead, she narrowed her eyes and stared me down.

"Why?"

"What do you mean, why?" I said. She apparently had never heard the saying about gift horses and not looking them in the mouth.

"Why did you advise Harriet to give the manuscript to us?"

I paused. "I didn't know very much about Jane Austen before I came to Oxford." I glanced around me. "Nothing, really, beyond *Pride and Prejudice* and some movie versions of her other books. I thought she just wrote some love stories, and that was pretty much it."

"And now?" Mrs. Parrot's eyebrows rose.

"I know her better. Not as much as you, or as some of these people." I waved a hand to indicate the people who were now moving through the courtyard. "I may never be a true scholar. But I think I've learned enough to know the most important thing about her."

"And what would that be?" Mrs. Parrot still looked skeptical.

"I think I have to trust that Austen knew her own mind as well as her heart. If she had wanted *First Impressions* to be public, she wouldn't have given it to Cassandra to destroy along with her letters. I think she wanted to give Mr. Darcy a chance to redeem himself. Or at least give herself a chance to redeem him."

"You don't think the world has a right to know of its existence?" She waved a hand at the manuscript.

I shrugged. "A right to know? Maybe. Or maybe not." I looked at her, struggling to find the words for what I was trying to say. "All I know is that you're the only one besides Harriet who didn't want to make a profit off of it. You're the only one who wanted to treasure it." I handed her the ribbon-wrapped pages. "You've been at this a lot longer than I have. Maybe someday you'll decide that it needs to be made known to the world. But for now, it's your secret to keep."

She took the manuscript from me, and I felt the loss of its weight more in my heart than in my hands. I also felt, at that moment, the strangest sense of connection with Jane Austen, as if I'd had at least a glimpse of what it must have been like when she herself turned over her letters and papers to her sister. I'd known she died at a young age, but until that moment, I hadn't realized how significant that fact was. She had been a woman in her prime, maybe ten years older than I was at that moment, struck down by illness, forced to rely on others to protect her privacy. She had known what she wanted her legacy to be and had acted accordingly, but the fate of her work hadn't been in her hands alone.

"Thank you," Mrs. Parrot said, and I could see the glimmer of tears in her eyes. She might be a Formidable, but she was a Formidable with a heart. "We will take good care of it."

"I know." And I did. And in that moment I also knew that since the death of my parents, I had acted as a sort of Formidable in my own right. I had done my best to protect my parents' legacy, to shelter Missy from the fallout of their deaths, and to keep our family together. But now it was time to let go. Perhaps I had more in common with Jane Austen than I would have ever guessed.

"Good-bye." I didn't offer her my hand, since hers were occupied with the manuscript.

"Good-bye, Miss Prescott." She nodded regally. "I hope you have a safe journey home."

"Thank you. You too," I said, and then I turned and walked away, knowing that Harriet would be pleased and that I had finally done the right thing.

⚜⚜⚜⚜⚜

I was waiting outside Tom Tower for my taxi when I saw Martin coming down St. Aldate's.

"Claire. I had hoped to see you again before you left." He smiled and reached for my hand. "I will miss you."

"Me too." I stepped forward and gave him an impulsive hug. "So much has happened..." I trailed off, not sure how much to say. "I just want to thank you for your help."

"Ah, yes, the mysterious pages." His eyes twinkled in their usual way.

"And what you said in the seminar yesterday too. About Jane Austen. It really helped."

He smiled. "I don't suppose you'd tell me the truth about those pages."

I smiled, too, but shook my head. "You were the one who said Oxford was full of secrets."

He laughed. "Yes, but I didn't mean that you should keep them from me." He took my hand in his. "I wish you all the best, Claire."

"And I wish the same for you." I squeezed his hand. "You know, there's something else I've been meaning to ask you."

"Yes?"

"I guess I was just wondering why you would come to a seminar like this. James said you were one of the leading Austen scholars in the world. Why hang out with a bunch of amateurs?"

He released my hand. "Do you know what the word *amateur* means? Literally?"

I shook my head.

"It means *one who loves*."

"One who loves?"

"I came here to be with people who read Jane Austen simply for the love of it. Not for academic reasons. Not for profit. Merely for the joy of her stories and her language."

"Oh." I hadn't thought of that. "So you came here for the fun of it?"

He laughed. "Precisely." And then his expression grew more serious. "You should come back next year. For the same reason."

I nodded. "Maybe I will." How long had it been since I'd done something just for the fun of it?

My taxi pulled up to the curb, and I reached for my suitcase. "Good-bye, Martin. I hope we meet again."

"Good-bye, Claire. I do too."

The driver loaded my suitcase into the taxi, and I slid inside. Here I was, right where I'd begun.

So much had happened in one short week. So much had changed. I'd never expected an adventure. Never wanted a challenge. But now I was so glad that I had found both. And I was even happier that I had proved to be worthy of them.

෴෴෴෴

The departure lounge at Heathrow was full by the time I arrived. I glanced around, hoping to spot an empty seat, when

I saw a familiar-looking Royals cap that had definitely seen better days.

Neil.

It couldn't be. But it was.

My first instinct was to hide, but obviously we were going to be on the same plane for a lot of hours. Plus, with my luck, he would have the seat next to me. I might as well face the inevitable.

I walked over to him and set down my carry-on.

"Hey," I said. "I thought you left yesterday."

"Hey," he replied and rose to his feet. "I was on standby and couldn't get on, so they put me up in a hotel for the night."

I would have liked to delude myself into thinking that he'd purposely manipulated matters so that we were on the same plane home, but I knew better.

We stood there in silence for several long, uncomfortable moments.

"I'm sorry." I took a step backward. "I didn't mean to disturb—"

"What did you want, Claire?" He shoved his hands into the pockets of his khaki shorts.

You, I wanted to say. *I want you*. But if I actually said those words…well, I didn't think they would be too well received.

"I just wanted to apologize one more time. For everything."

He took off the cap and scratched the back of his head.

His hair stood on end in unaccustomed disorder. "You did that already. In Oxford."

"I know, but—"

"How's James?"

The question caught me off guard. "James? He's—"

"Rich? Good looking? A big improvement over a jock like me?"

His words hit me like a blow, and I winced, not so much from their power but from the realization that he was very, very angry. He slammed the cap back on his head.

"Sorry, Claire. I shouldn't have said that. No matter what's happened between us." He let out a gusty sigh. "I knew all along I wasn't the right man for you. Guess I thought if I ignored it, then it wouldn't be true."

"But—"

"James is a lucky guy. Tell him I said so." He fixed his gaze on a spot somewhere over my shoulder.

"Neil—"

His face softened a little. "I'll be okay, Claire. So will you."

Which wasn't true, of course. Well, it might have been true for him, but it definitely wasn't true for me.

"Neil, wait—"

He shook his head. "I already have, Claire. For a lot longer than I should have."

"I know." I stepped toward him, wishing I still had the right to reach for his hand. To hold it in mine. Although at that moment I would have done a lot more clutching than holding. "I've been an idiot," I said, and tears stung my eyes.

He smiled, but his expression was filled with sadness, not humor. "That makes two of us." He hesitated, as if he wanted to say something else. That hesitation lit a very fragile flame of hope in the space where my heart had been.

It was time to swallow whatever pride I had left. "I thought you should know that I realize I made a huge mistake."

His chin lifted several inches. "What kind of mistake?"

"Well, more than one mistake, of course, but the biggest one was this." I reached into my pocket and pulled out the box that held the engagement ring. I opened it, and it sparkled under the fluorescent lighting.

Neil scowled. "Thanks a lot, Claire."

"No, no. You don't understand." Alarm and adrenaline flooded through me. "The mistake wasn't you." I stopped and swallowed in an effort to get the words past the lump in my throat. "The mistake was not realizing how much I love you."

I couldn't believe I had actually said the words, but judging from the expression on his face, I must have. I saw disbelief. Comprehension. Confusion. Anger. And then the very faintest beginning of what I'd been hoping for, what I'd been longing to see.

Joy. The tiniest spark, deep in his eyes.

"Claire—" The word held a warning note.

"Wait. Let me say the whole speech."

"You prepared a speech?"

"I didn't sleep much last night."

"All right. Let's hear it."

"I blamed you." Okay, maybe not the best start, but at least I was trying. Neil made a half-strangled noise but didn't say anything. I screwed up my courage and continued.

"You weren't anything like what I thought a hero should be, even though you were everything I wanted. Well, almost everything. I still thought something was missing. It was easier to blame you for spending too much time watching ball games and taking me for granted than to deal with my own problems, to accept that you got tired of making plans and my canceling them so I could go running over to Missy's house."

The joy began to drain out of his face, so I rushed headlong into the final part of my speech.

"Then, when I met James in Oxford, I thought he was the man I'd been waiting for. A hero right out of Austen. The one who would finally make everything okay. Only he wasn't real." I wiped away the tears that swam in my eyes. "Like Austen's characters, he was just fiction. Mr. Darcy broke my heart."

Neil took a step toward me, but I held up a hand to stop him.

"I didn't know love could be soft and subtle and still be strong as steel," I said. "I kept waiting for the grand entrance, the fireworks, and the trumpet fanfare. I didn't know it could be like this." And then I stepped toward him. I placed my hands gently on either side of his face. He hadn't shaved in a while, and his cheeks were rough beneath my fingers.

I kissed him and held my breath at the same time. The combination of his lips and my lack of oxygen weakened my knees. I swayed. His arms came up to catch me and then enfolded me.

"Claire—"

"I know you can't forgive me." I sagged against him, grateful for that one last moment of his body pressed against mine. "I wouldn't expect you to. I just wanted you to know that... well, that I *know*. Now. That I figured out the difference. Even if it is too late."

I pushed against his chest, eager to make my getaway now that I'd delivered my speech. But his arms tightened, and suddenly I couldn't catch my breath even when I was trying.

"What makes you think it's too late?" He practically growled the words in my ear. I closed my eyes and tried to pretend that I hadn't heard them.

"But you said—"

"You're not the only one who can be a fool."

He kissed me then. A kiss worthy of every incarnation of Mr. Darcy that ever existed, whether on the page, stage, or screen. If he hadn't been holding me up, I would have melted into a puddle right there in the departure lounge.

"June 3," I murmured against his lips. He drew his head back.

"What?"

"June 3. It was my parents' anniversary."

He eyed me with caution. "So?"

"I think it should be our anniversary too."

He was silent for a long time, and my heart rate, which had slowed a little, now accelerated again. Maybe I had misunderstood. Maybe he couldn't forgive me after all. Maybe—

"Do you even know what day of the week it falls on next summer?"

"It's on a Saturday. I checked. Although that gives me less than a year to plan the wedding."

"You already looked at a calendar?"

I nodded.

I stepped back and glanced down at the engagement ring, the box still cupped in my hand. "Unless, of course, you want this back."

He nodded. "I do want it back."

My stomach tightened in a knot, but then he took the box from me, took the ring out of it, and reached for my left hand. "Claire, will you marry me?"

At my tearful nod, he slid the ring on my finger.

"I'm no Mr. Darcy," he whispered, and he pulled me back into his arms. "I'll still watch way too many ball games and feed you takeout."

I laughed. "I know. And I'll still run sometimes, at the drop of a hat, when Missy needs me."

He smoothed back the strands of hair that had fallen across my cheek. "The most important thing is that I'll be here. I'm not going anywhere."

I chuckled. "Actually, you are."

"I am?"

"Yes," I said, and I kissed him again. "You're going home with me."

He laughed. "I think it's about time."

And he was right. It was.

Author's Note

Jane Austen wrote the original version of *Pride and Prejudice*, called *First Impressions*, by the time she was twenty-one. It was only years later, when she finally settled at Chawton with her mother and sister, that she returned to the manuscript and rewrote it in the form we have today. That much is true.

The Formidables and their secrets are entirely a product of my imagination, but it's not beyond the realm of possibility that Austen's lost manuscript might one day come to light. The version of *First Impressions* in this novel is, of course, entirely fictional.

Reading Group Guide

1. Claire Prescott realizes that she has put her sister first in everything because she has been afraid to live her own life. At what point does sacrificing for the people we love become more hurtful than helpful? How do we know when we have crossed that line? How can we restore those relationships to a healthier balance?

2. The plot of the novel revolves around the keeping of secrets. How do you know when to keep a secret and when to share it? What are the risks of keeping secrets? What are the benefits?

3. When she arrives in Oxford, Claire decides to recreate herself. To do so, though, she must deceive the people she meets. Do you think it's understandable that she would fall prey to this temptation? What price does she pay for her duplicity?

4. In the end, do you think Claire gave Harriet the right advice about what to do with the manuscript? Why or why not? If you had been in Harriet's place, what decision would you have made?

5. In recent years, Mr. Darcy has truly become an iconic romantic hero. Do you think he is a true hero? Why or why not? If you had been Claire, would you have chosen James or Neil? In your estimation, what makes a man a hero?